Discords of The Mind Vol. 1
A Collection of Short Stories

Stories By BC. Neon, Edited By Sean Ailshie

An imprint of BC. Neon

ISBN 978-1-9543-8901-4 (Soft Cover)
ISBN 978-1-9543-8900-7 (Hard Cover)
ISBN 978-1-9543-8902-1 (eBook)

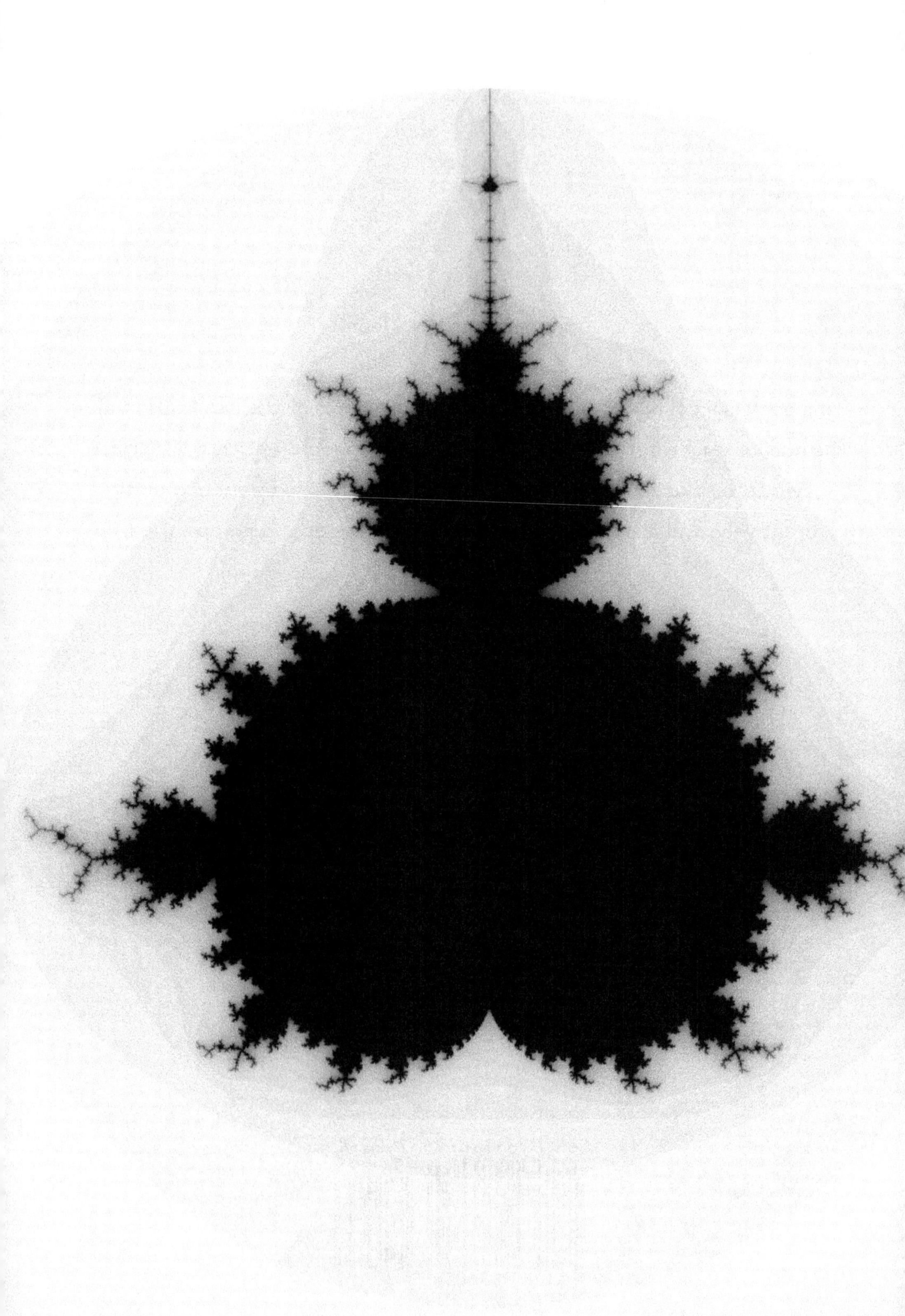

About The Cover

The Mandelbrot Set is a mathematical figure, not an ink blot, with infinite detail, both on the surface and hidden inside the volume (also referred to as the Buddhabrot Set). You can find many mathematical anomalies such as π, e, self-similar structures, or approximations of another set of sets named The Filled Julia Sets in the structures and details on and in the Mandelbrot set.

Similar to the rendition on the cover, my writing style lacks the fine descriptions and details you may find in other books and stories (or other Mandelbrot Sets) so that you may imagine the fine details of the following stories for yourself and experience the stories in your own unique way.

Please Enjoy.

Table Of Contents

Angels

⊪◎⊫

"LOCK DOWN TIME, son," my father tells me, "Close your windows, and make sure they're locked this time."

"Yessir, father," I repeat back to him.

I shut the window, cutting off the cool night breeze. The glow of military spotlights light up the sky like clockwork. They highlight the silhouette of a single demon flying through the sky.

"I remember their first attack," father goes on, "I was an emergency surgeon for the wounded; utter savages."

"You've told me before," I tell him. He pats my back and walks over to his study to review patient files before heading to work.

Suddenly, the shadow of the demon gets snatched out of the sky. "I wonder what did that," I say under my breath to myself.

"What was that son?" he calls out to me.

"Nothing," I reply.

"Thought so..."

The painful cries of a woman pierce the night, followed by the echo of metallic ringing. Must be the military hunting down the animals. The ringing and screams of pain continue throughout the night. My father finally pulls the cord to the lamp, darkening the rest of the house, and leaves to work at the hospital. I count the moments until I know he's gone so I can sneak out.

I grab the toy gun under my mattress and rush to the front door. The locks slide open, and I run out the door, assured that the door will close and lock itself.

"H-hey, dude, I hear if you hit the horns hard enough, it'll break off just like a deer's," I overhear in the distance, followed by the loud metal ringing and a scream of pain.

I follow the sounds, but all I find are some hooligans beating a female demon they snatched from the air. I announce my presence by making a clicking noise with my mouth to imitate the gun.

"Hey, bro, no need for that," one of the thugs tells me, dropping his metal pipe and raising his arms, "We ain't got time for that, let's go."

The thugs back away into the night and I hear them scurry off when they're out of sight. "Holy moly," I say aloud staring at the stubby, gazelle-like horns, "You're, like, a real demon."

She starts trying to break through the net one knot at a time, making very slow progress. I notice her sharp claw-like fingernails and reddish skin under the streetlight. "You're going to need help with that," I say, slowly approaching her.

"Go away," she says, stopping me in my tracks.

"You can speak, that's good to know," I think aloud, "Those weights are magnetic and are held down by the rebar in the ground."

She rips through one of the knots, "I'm well aware. Now leave."

I drop the toy gun and slowly approach the net. I try to get a good look at her, but my heart is pounding. All I can see is a very pretty woman.

"Leave!" she shouts.

"You have a broken hand, I'm going to help," I persist onward, pulling one the weights upward. The magnetic field separates from the rebar and flings upward, knocking my chin. She grabs around and tries the pull herself away from the net, but one of her horns catches.

"I'll get that—"

She stands up, and her wings push all the weights from the concrete. "Leave!" she shouts at me, spreading her wings wide, and heaving the net away. I become engulfed in fear, falling back to the ground.

"Holy crap!" The net falls back down, snagging on a horn and pulls her down to the concrete directly on her right wing. *CRACK!* She screams bloody murder in pain as her wing breaks, and her head smashes against the ground.

"Uh," I freeze, "You need a doctor; now."

"I told you to go," she manages to say through the intense pain, spitting out a little blood, "Are you stupid?"

"No, I'm not stupid, but you just broke a bone," I look at a severely swollen hand, "More than one bone, and I can take you to a doctor."

"I don't need any of your help," she says, "I just need to go back home!" She manages to crawl her way out of the net and stand. I can see the pain she's in as she spreads her wings, which sends her back to her knees.

"I know a doctor who can help you."

She glares at me with fierce yellow-colored eyes, but bows her head in acceptance of my offer. I outstretch my hand, but she bats it away, scratching my hand a little.

"Just follow me then," I instruct her, "If you are going to be like that."

"I don't need human pity," she barks at me.

"It's not pity, just goodwill."

We begin to move down into the alleyways; the female demon follows, folding her wings close, squeezing into the tight space between the two buildings.

"So what's your name?" I ask.

"Shut up," she replies.

"I'm just trying not to be—"

"I said shut up, how truly stupid are people here?"

"Ouch," I say, "I mean, I know some stupid people, but an entire species isn't stupid."

"You wouldn't consider a dog smart, would you?"

I think back to a childhood friend, and his dog. "Well, I had a friend whose dog could open doors."

"Not," she pauses, giving me a sense of anger, "relevant."

"There's a hospital nearby, I can sneak in through the back," I tell her, "I know a doctor that'll help you."

She stops before the street light illuminates her. "Well, come on!" I persist, waving my hand in the direction of the hospital.

"I'm not exactly well-liked by human people," she warns me.

"I scared those thugs away, take a chill."

"Take a what?" she asks.

I roll my eyes and wave my hand dismissively. "Figure of speech."

We try to sneak to the back door of a joint quick care and dentistry where my father works. The lock on the door is entirely worn out and I press down with all my weight to slip the mechanism. I hear some people walking and conversing, but I listen carefully to make sure they're gone.

"Come on," I order her.

She fumbles through the door with her large wing broken out of shape. A few nurses from the quick care see her and they scream and retreat back down the hall.

I lead her into the doctor's office that I know very well: my father's. I used to be very reckless as a child, so I would sneak into his office where he would physically chastise me and give me the care I needed. I expect this time to be no different.

I lead her down the hall to his office, where I'm greeted by him reviewing more patient files. "Why are you here Ostin?" he asks, "What could you have possibly done now?"

"Someone needs help—"

"Then they should've checked into the front," he angrily replies.

The female demon shoves past me and slams her claws into the desk, through the stack of papers. "Fix me," she demands

He remains calm in the face of danger, "Very well. What ails you?"

She shows him her swollen and bloodied hand. He reaches out and starts pressing his fingers into her wrist as she winces in pain. "You've dislocated some of your wrist bones," he says, right before forcing the bones back in place.

She screams and falls to her knees while getting ready to strike. Miraculously, her hand begins to recede to normal size. "On your knees, as you should be, hybrid scum," he comments, "I'll need to stabilize the bones back into place on your wing."

She shoots back to her feet with her fingers straightened out like spears right under his chin. "Do it, or I *will* kill you."

He reaches over for his desk stapler. "Allow me." her hand lowers and he firmly grasps the bone on her back before forcing it upright. As she screams, he jams the staple around the break until it's like tough cables holding up a bridge.

She falls to the ground once more in pain as her hand reaches for her wing, writhing around. I look at her face, dark red tears flowing from her eyes. "Now get the hell away from here," father commands, going to sit back at his desk, reaching underneath to sound the alarm.

She stumbles to her feet and pushes me away, making her way outside. I chase after her, but I see her take off into the night before I make it to her. I look back to see my father's angry, stern stare. "Go home, Ostin," he commands. I wander back home, preparing myself for the punishment I'm sure to receive.

❮❙ ⊙ ❙❯

SLAP! The knuckles leave a stinging sensation and the noise leaves a ringing in my ear. "Do you have any idea what kind of danger you put everyone in?" he shouts, "I've told you countless times, are you too stupid to understand?"

I haven't seen him this angry in a while. *SLAP!* He hits me again, this time cutting my cheek on my tooth. That was a very painful Thursday night for me. The military came and shut down my father's practice for a week or so to investigate, but I'm sure nothing came of it. I've thought about that demon quite a bit lately; I'm not sure exactly what I expected, but she definitely was something different.

A gust of wind blows in my face, forcing my eyes shut and miss that last sliver of light before sunset. I attempt to walk inside the house and lock both the deadbolts, but I'm interrupted by the bellowing flaps of someone familiar. "Oh, no," I say to myself.

I turn around to see two female demons, the one from three weeks ago, and a new one. Panicking, I try to rush inside, but the new demon presses her hand against the door. "Don't run," she tells me, standing a few inches above me, "Well, Martta?"

I begin to hyperventilate and try to pull the door open when the new demon lightly slaps my cheek a few times. "Calm down, will you?" she commands me.

"What are you guys doing here?" I say, "There's military everywhere!"

The blonde one replies, "In our culture, we're not supposed to leave a good deed unpaid, it's bad luck."

The other one bows very formally. "Thank you for your kindness," she grits, "I am Martta."

"Yeah, hi," I say, "Name's Ostin, why exactly are you here?"

Martta lifts her head and scowls at me. "Kiira just told you."

"Okay, right," I start to panic again, "You're going to get captured if you don't leave—"

Martta lunges at me, slamming me into the door and slicing my chest with her claws, followed by the boom of my father's shotgun. The slug flies through the railing and into the roof.

"We're leaving now!" Kiira shouts as she climbs onto the roof.

Martta begins climbing over me when a slug fires itself next to her leg. "Wait! I have questions," I call out.

She glares back down at me and says, "Say nothing."

The sounds of police sirens get louder as they approach the house. I look up at the roof and they're gone. Not a moment later, the military burst through the balcony door waving their guns around like they're toys.

"You okay, boy?" one of them asks. I nod feeling the cuts left by Martta. I look through the guardrail to see my father laying down his shotgun. "It's okay," I yell out, "You didn't shoot me."

It took several hours for them to comb through the house before they started to even try to interrogate me like I had expected. I had to wait around for hours with three soldiers with big guns. Finally, a man in a loose-fitting black suit steps out of one of the vehicles.

"How are you doing today, son?" he asks me.

I scratch around the cuts to try to alleviate some discomfort. "I've had better days, I suppose."

He pulls out a notepad and a very expensive-looking pen. "I'm going to need some straight answers from you, no supposing."

"I guess," I tell him, and he looks up at me slightly annoyed.

"You have any idea why the demons came after you specifically?" he asks.

"No, not really," I lie to him.

"No, or not really?" he persists.

"No."

"Would you be able to identify the two demons if you were shown a database of known creatures?" he continues.

"I didn't really get a good look at him." A database? I wonder how much the military knows about all this. After all, all this has been going since before I was born.

He keeps on writing in the notepad. "Can you describe the two demons in any detail? Along with the one you encountered at your father's practice?" Who's giving them all this? I suppose they have to have somebody, it *is* the military.

"I don't really remember the one from three weeks ago, and I didn't get a good look at these ones either," I lie again, "It all happened pretty quickly."

"Alright, thank you," he clicks his pen, "You and your father are going to have to be under our protection for the time being until we further evaluate this threat."

"Okay," I respond, "When?"

"In thirty minutes."

"Do I get to bring anything with me—"

"For your personal safety, no," he says before closing the door to his blacked-out vehicle. Soon enough, I start seeing everybody here disappear behind cold steel doors, and I'm eventually herded into one such vehicle as well.

I look around the armored inside to see which one of these people will answer any of my questions while I adjust the seat belt for comfort on my chest. "How long is this going to take?" I ask.

"Classified," one of them responds.

"Where are we—"

"Classified," he replies again.

The vehicle jostles around for a moment like it was hit with something or ran over a large animal. "What on earth was that—"

"Classified."

"Of course it is," I say.

After hours of classified silence, the armored van comes to a halt. The doors swing open revealing blinding white lights and concrete walls. Mr. Classified unbuckles me and they lead me down a hall into a pseudo prison cell. "Strip naked and leave *everything* on the table, there are new clothes on the bed."

Mr. Classified walks out and the thick mechanical door slides shut. I start emptying my pockets and I look down at my phone; crushed and shattered. One long, painful sigh later, I put on the clothes.

⊷⊙⊶

Say nothing. That was very hard to do during my stay.

"Do you recognize any of these demons?" He asks, handing me a tablet with multiple photos, "This is a list of the sixteen most likely demons to be in that area on that day."

I look through them, and I see Kiira among the faces. Demons look a lot like people. They have different, reddish skin tones and facial structures like us. Their horns are very different from each other, though.

"I don't recognize any of them," I say, giving the computer back.

"Are you sure? This information is critical."

"None of them ring a bell."

"You may be too young to remember when all this started," he sits down, and sets the tablet on the table, "We are at war. They punched a hole in time and space just to come here and kill everything in sight."

"I told you," I repeat, "I don't recognize any of them."

"You looked at CN197 for a bit longer than the others," he enlarges Kiira's image, "This demon was confirmed to be within ten miles of your residence that night.

"And she was seen with another female demon, not on record. The only other demon seen in that area at that time was AA324."

I look at him, and lie again, "I've never seen her."

"We know you're lying," he approaches me, "Your father was able to recognize CN197 as one of the demons on your balcony.

"Why are you protecting them?"

"I don't recognize them," I persist, "It happened very quickly."

"Your father accounted that you had a brief conversation with the demons before he opened fire at them. Can you recall that conversation?"

My irritation grows out of control. "You know what? I'm not going to tell you. I don't have to."

He calmly says, "This is a matter of national security."

"I don't care," I tell him.

He ponders on my words for a brief moment. "Very well. I'll see that you and your father be sent home as soon as possible."

And that was that, the last time I spoke to someone in this classified location. The next day we were transported back home in a blacked-out limousine. That ride was a very awkward experience considering my father was on the verge of beating me again, and there was another guy in a loose suit sitting on the opposite set of seats. Nothing was said the entire time.

The home was as it was left, with a new patch of grass and dustier with a couple of things knocked on their sides, but now the floor is wet from the water we tracked in from the rain. As soon as the front door closes, father turns around and backhands me with all his might throwing me to the ground.

"The hell were you thinking?" he shouts.

Words try to come out, but they don't from fear and Pavlov training, but I hear a roughly familiar voice.

"Don't do that to him," Martta tells him, but nowhere to be seen.

I look around to find the source of her voice and find Martta, dressed in a leather tunic and what looks to be brown denim.

"And what are you doing here?" father asks her, collecting himself from his exertions.

"You nearly shot me," she explains, "I don't take very kindly to that."

"Consider that payment for medical coercion," he retorts back.

She gives one short laugh. "I came for something, and you're going to give it to me."

"I'd rather die," he shouts.

Martta readies her claws. "Don't tempt me."

"Can you both just calm down?" I say, wiping blood from my mouth.

Father glares at me. "You need to shut the hell up, Ostin."

Martta lunges toward father, and grabs him by surprise by the throat.

"There was something buried in the ground by your house. Tell me where it is."

"Over my dead body," father grabs a nearby glass bottle and breaks it over her horn.

She rotates her head back and tightens her grip, "Where did they take it?"

Martta squeezes her nails into his flesh, forcing blood to flow down into his clothes. "They moved it to a *secure* location that you'll never find," he manages to say.

She tosses him aside into the table. "Do you know where it is?"

"Can't say that I do," I say backing away from her, "I thought you guys couldn't be in sunlight."

"Who lied to you?" she snarks.

"Well, I mean," I explain, "you guys usually come about when the sun sets."

She rolls her eyes and begins to walk away.

"Wait!" I call out, "I still have questions!"

"You get one question, and I have to leave," she turns back around, "That's a courtesy, and it's already too dangerous."

"What are you doing here?" I catch my breath from standing up.

"I'm looking for something," she scoffs, walking away.

I think back to all those pictures of demons that they made me look through. "They know who Kiira is."

She stops abruptly. "What?"

"They took me, and tried to have me point you and Kiira out from a bunch of pictures of you guys."

She lunges to me and pulls me with her as she leaves from the house. Martta rushes out the door and bear-hugs me as she begins to flap her wings through the rain. Moments later, we're gliding through the light rain, with all the pins and needles of the raindrops smacking my face at high speeds.

"What on earth are you doing?" I speak above the rain, "Where are you taking me?"

"Shut up!" she shouts back to me.

I try to look to the ground to see that she's flying out of town, to the forest. "Why'd you take me?"

"I said to shut up," she yells out, "Take my advice."

I notice a tree zoom past us, and another. And all of a sudden, I can't see the sky anymore, or the city for that matter. She comes to a sudden stop, flinging me across the wet forest ground.

"What do you mean," she begins to rush towards me, "That they have a database of demons?"

I crawl up to a nearby tree. "They had me look through a bunch of photos of known demons. They all had photos and code names."

"They know about Kiira?" she asks, lifting me by my shirt.

"Yeah, she was listed on there, and they know that she was at my house that night."

"How?!" she screams.

My latent fear of heights finally hits me, "I don't know, it's the military."

She lets go, and screeches in a particular way, the wildlife goes rampant.

Oh man, I might die tonight, I think to myself. Martta turns around and punches the tree adjacent to herself. Familiar sounds of flapping wings greet my ears again.

"What's going on?" Kiira asks Martta, "And why is he here again?"

"They know about us," she sulkily says.

"Explain this," she points her finger at me.

"They have a very long list of the ones we've sent out here, maybe more."

"Damn," Kiira mutters under her breath, "You found out from him?"

I nod my head, "Yeah, I told her. They had me look through a bunch of photos with assigned numbers to them."

Martta screams again. "And they moved it."

"So it was buried by his home all this time?"

Martta nods. "I watched them remove it from the ground. I tried to follow where they were taking it as far as I could without being seen."

"This is bad—" Kiira pauses, and her eyes widen, "Hide!"

Kiira immediately launches off and glides away into the treetops. A huge wire net is launched and wraps around the tree, glancing my head. I move my eyes to Martta, and see, in almost slow motion, a similar net launching at her. The net wraps around her and knocks her to the ground. A flash of light goes off and I hear the brief crackling of an electric shock.

"No!" I reach out, being knocked over myself with a wire net. "Martta!" I shout, readying myself for the electric shock.

But the shock never comes and I see the hoards of soldiers marching into the forest, armed with guns.

"Found them!" someone shouts out.

◂◦▸

The light switches on with a loud *CLICK*, leaving a ringing in my ears followed by the blinding white light. My eyes adjust to see yet another man in a loose-fitting suit sitting down across from this steel table I'm handcuffed to.

"You've gotten yourself into some trouble with the U.S. government," he begins to say.

"I've done nothing wrong, so you can just—"

"I'll be deciding what we'll do here," he continues, "As far as we're concerned, you've been conspiring with the worst enemy man has ever seen; that's a federal offense."

"I'm not conspiring with anyone."

"We may not be in any active battles," he says, "But let me assure you, Ostin, we are still under martial law and at war."

"I am not conspiring with anyone," I angrily space out my words.

He takes a deep breath in and out. "Your father reported that you brought a demon into his medical practice where he was coerced into providing it medical treatment. It later protected you from your abusive father, attacking with extreme bias. That, Ostin, is enough to send you to federal prison as an adult."

"So she has a decent conscience," I explain, "That doesn't mean I've been conspiring—"

"More evidence," he pulls out a familiar tablet, "You were cited having an extended conversation with one about a month ago—"

I stand up and try to pull my hands up too. "They came to me!" I yell.

He stands as well, slamming his hands on the table, "Do you expect me to believe these are people, Ostin?!" he quickly sits back down and I hear some loud chatter coming from his earpiece.

"You referred to one of the demons as 'Martta.' Is that her name?"

I lump back into the cold, steel chair. "I guess, she came to me and gave me this whole 'in my culture' talk and flew off."

He pauses, leaving the sound of more chatter in his earpiece. After an uncomfortably long pause of silence, he says, "And do you know anything about their culture?"

"No," I tell him, "No, I do not."

There's more radio chatter, until he asks, "Can you tell me the name of the other demon that escaped the other day?"

"Yeah, Kiira; I think you guys call her CN197." He promptly stands up and rushes out the door, and as he walks out another man in another loose-fitting suit with sunglasses walks in. "Is there anything else you can tell us?" he asks in a plain, static voice.

"Yeah, can you guys not afford better fitting clothes?" I retort.

He sighs, briskly walks over to the table and releases my handcuffs. "Follow me."

He pulls me around the table and along with him, passing me off to one of the soldiers. We walk down what seems to be an infinite concrete hallway until we finally reach the end. The man turns around and lowers his sunglasses, revealing cold blue eyes. "We would be willing to forgive your," he pauses, "*Federal* crimes—"

"I did nothing wrong in the first—" I try to say.

"If you can get more information out of these creatures." He slides a card next to the door, followed by the thuds of massive locks moving around the inside of the walls. One of the soldiers flicks on the lights and I'm again blinded by a bright fluorescent white. I look around to see Martta thrashing around in a cage with a tight jacket around her wings. One of the soldiers jams an electrode into her side, making her scream.

I look back over to the man. "This is wrong and you know—" I tell him.

"They're not people, Ostin; they're hybrid scum," he says, pushing his sunglasses back up. He pushes me into the room and the door closes. I try to push the door open, but the vault-like door locks into place.

Martta screams in pain, thrashing around violently as I look around for something other than concrete walls and steel. Eventually, I find a cable running from the cage to the wall with a mysterious wire cutter sitting next to it. I rush to go cut the wire, and as I sink the cutters into the wire of the cage, a powerful jolt rushes through my arms, knocking me backward and numbing my entire body.

Martta is still thrashing around, but less violently. "Calm down," I groan, "I'll get you out of that as soon as I start feeling my hands." She still doesn't stop but slows to speak.

"What did they tell you to do to me?" she demands, finally stopping and sitting down inside the cage. I roll over to my side to look her in the eyes as we speak.

"Nothing really, they just kind of shoved me in here," I reply in pain. I find the strength to crawl over and start snipping the wires to the electrical net to free her, but she keeps moving around.

"Why do you keep helping me?" she demands to know again.

"You seem to need—"

"Don't you know what I am to you?"

I shake my head, "I was born after all that. All I know is my dad keeps telling me he was drafted as a trauma surgeon."

She scoffs and finally settles down enough for me to keep cutting the net off. "You know literally nothing."

"My father keeps me isolated from people and the media, so no," I reply, "No school or anything."

"What's 'school' mean?" she asks.

"It's a place where people go to learn."

I snip the last wire and she lunges at me, trying to escape the cage and scaring the daylights out of me. "Why do you let people hit you and push you around?"

"I'm a child, there's, uh, natural order to things around here—"

"That would never happen in *my* home!" she shouts in an odd way, maybe to lure the men in suits out to her.

"They are listening—"

"I'm counting on that," she says, trying to pull the cage bars apart, "I'll claw my way out of here if I need to."

After hours of Martta saying things to try and make them come out, the locks to move and a single gun barrel pokes through the opening, followed by another soldier after it's fully open.

One of the soldiers starts handling me by my handcuffs, whilst the other keeps aiming at Martta, who's trying to claw and taunt him through the cage.

"Let me out of here!" She says, "I'll beat you to death."

They start to pull me out of the room with me resisting and the last thing I see before being pulled around the corner is a tranquilizer flying into her outreached hand.

⫷ ⊙ ⫸

Martta slowly opens her eyes after being knocked unconscious, but quickly closes them under the harsh white light. For a moment, she's tranquil but starts thrashing around once again in her straitjacket. I've been handcuffed to the floor this entire time while she has been sleeping. They forced me into new clothes, but these ones are strange, needing to be tied in the front and the back like a Mexican poncho, but cut way too much on the back, seemingly for extra limbs.

She starts yelling out violently; I can see her arms and wings twitching around underneath the fabric. After a few minutes, she begins to slow down, but she starts to tear up with blood in her eyes. "I'm really going to die here," she whimpers to herself, "It's all my fault too."

"Who said they're not going to let you out?" I ask her.

She says something under her breath, seemingly in her own language. "At least you're still here with me."

The blood-tears drip down her face onto the straitjacket. "They probably put you in there because they thought you were going to attack someone—"

She falls to the ground and screams. "I was," she confesses in a quiet voice, "How long have I been here?"

"A couple of hours; they shot you with a tranquilizer and almost knocked me out the old-fashioned way when I cut you out of that net."

She bangs her forehead on the ground a few times. "I don't know what that means," she says quietly, "You're always trying to help, just leave!"

I move around to try and get comfortable on this cold concrete floor. "So, here's what they told me, Martta—"

"Don't say my name," she interrupts.

"They're going to let us out of here if I get you to answer a bunch of questions they want." I try to lean over to my hands to scratch my nose. "Something to give them an advantage against you guys."

"What more advantage do they want," she replies, "You already have machines beyond our own. We're both going to die in here.

"You're an imbecile!" she yells, "We're both going to die!"

Confusion enters my mind of what they want me to ask, and my face shows it. "I doubt that; you're an asset and my father has military connections."

Her yellow colored eyes lock onto me like a hawk. "They're going to torture and kill me like all the rest."

A voice starts talking in my ear, scaring me. I jump, but my hands pull me back down. I hear the voice say, "Make sure she doesn't injure herself."

Her eyes widen and her brow furls, "What did he say."

The voices come back, "She's a prime asset for experimentation; keep her in a good condition." I try to reach up to pull out the speaker in my ear, but the chains keep me restricted.

"I'll kill all of you!" she screams, lunging at me like an animal, "I'll murder all of you!"

The chain anchor on her back snaps tight, knocking the wind out of her and pulling her back. "You disgust me, Ostin."

The radio talks again, saying, "Tell her to calm down."

"Or what!" she shouts, followed by an electrical shock, knocking her to the ground.

"Or that, I guess," I say, "Are you okay?"

"I'm fine," she grunts, worming around to get comfortable.

My brain scatters around on what they want me to ask; do I ask about Hell or other demons?

"So," I trail off, "What's Hell like?"

Her face becomes noticeably angry, with the dried tears completing the horrifying look. "My home-world is called Ouauoa, it is not called Hell," she says, enunciating each word, "at least in my language."

"Your language?" I ask.

"What, do you think everyone speaks English in the universe?" she retorts, "Arrogant speck."

"How do you know English then?"

"My mother spoke English."

"Wait," I say, "Isn't your mother a demon too?"

She turns her head away. "Your arrogance is amazing."

The radio starts making noise again. "Ask about her mother."

She obviously hears it and curls up tightly. "Why do you want to know that? You would think human sacrifice would already be on their list."

I'm surprised by this, shaking my head. "I'm sorry?" I ask.

"Stop talking to me," she commands me.

⊷ ⊙ ⊶

My groggy eyes slowly open from exhaustive sleep, this time there's a table between Martta and myself, and a single plate of food. I reach up to scratch my face to reveal a much longer chain on the ground.

"Martta?" I ask aloud, trying to see if she's still there. I stand up to see her curled up in the corner, "Martta?"

"What do you want?" she retorts to me, angry as the day is long.

"There's food here if you want it," I say, followed by my own stomach growling at me to eat, "What kinds of things do you eat, on, uh, Oahu?"

"It's pronounced Ouauoa," she barks.

"My bad." I hear a defeated sigh from across the white-walled room.

"Yousi is the most popular for my people to eat," she confesses, sitting back up in the straitjacket to get comfortable. I see her face, covered in dark red smears all over.

"What is it," I ask.

"You'd call it a bird, it flies around fields where we grow our food," she tells.

"That is so incredibly—" she interrupts me as I pick up the fork.

"Just stop," she says, "Just stop talking."

The radio in my ear scares me with static. "Keep talking," they tell me.

"I *can* hear them very clearly," she sniffles.

"I think that's the point."

"They'll come for me," she says, "Kiira won't let me rot in here."

The radio starts to emit static again, with faint voices in the background. I look over to Martta to see here curling up, nodding her head back and forth to the noise. Finally, the voices come back, "Tell her there are currently one hundred and thirty-one demons in custody and experimentation."

Her head pops up, her eyes fiercely focusing on me. "What did they just say?"

I stand up and start backing away to the wall. "Martta, they're trying to make you lose your cool."

She stands up and marches forward to me as I am slowly backing up. "It's working," she says, right as her chain snaps tight, "I will kill every last one of them, Ostin, I'll do it with my bare hands. If they're too afraid, I'll burrow through these walls to reach them."

She circles back around to get her horn right into one of the chain links, and pulls forward. *SNAP!* The chain breaks and she marches right to me, pushing me right up against the corner. She whispers, "Come get me."

She backs away and starts thrashing around in the jacket. Her limbs wiggle around underneath the fabric and the faint sounds of breaking stitches grow more and more frequent. She starts yelling, whether in pain or frustration when the fabric finally rips open; her hand flings about spraying blood all over the wall.

She screeches a particular sound I've never heard before and she starts trying to fimble the other sleeve open with nail-less fingers.

"Oh, my," I say to myself. She manages to tear open the other sleeve, nails intact this time. "Are you okay?"

"Are you okay—" she mocks me holding her hand in pain.

"Calm her down," the radio reminds me. In a violent rage, Martta throws the table at the wall, a plate of food with it. She marches up and pulls the radio from my ear, scratching my face up a little.

She stares me down, eye to eye as she breaks the radio with her fingers. "Get this off of me," she says.

"Uh, sure thing," I say, right before I fall down from the electric shock. My muscles contract and force my arms close to me in sharp pain. Suddenly, it stops. I look up and see Martta with one half of the chain.

"Oh," I grunt in pain, "Thanks for that." I manage to get on my feet and I start fiddling around with the final lock on her straitjacket. I press my thumb in between two pieces of metal when suddenly an intercom speaks up. I flinch at the sudden noise and break the final lock.

She starts removing the jacket, forcing me to cover my eyes. I hear the heavy metal and fabric hit the ground and a few joints crack. "What are you doing?" she asks.

"It's not okay to watch people change their clothes here, it's—"

"Then give me yours," she demands, and I hurry to get my shirt off. I toss it in her general direction, and I hear, "Thanks."

After a moment, I hear, "You can look now."

"Thank goodness," I say. Her wings spread and her horns point upwards. The image is magnificent. I notice her shirt is covered in blood already from cleaning her face.

"Come get me!" She shouts as the door locks start moving inside the walls. A gun barrel pokes through, but she grabs it and bends it around the corner. Another soldier comes through the opening doors, but she claws out his throat, knocking him to the ground.

This'll ruin my father if word gets out, I think to myself. Another man gets the better of Martta and puts her into a chokehold. "What are you going to do about it, Ostin?" he says.

I look down and pick up one of the guns as she thrashes around in the hold. I aim, close my eyes and pull the trigger. The noises stop and I look to see the man losing consciousness from the tranquilizers. Martta starts catching her breath and looks down the open door to her freedom.

She grabs my hand and pulls me along the way the oddly open hallways. We run down all the way to the last glass door. She kicks it open and all the people on the other side pause it astonishment.

"Get them!" a man in a loose black suit shouts, waving his hands around at us. A couple of men with guns rush towards, and I try and fire a few more tranquilizers at them while she charges the man in the suit.

I get both the guys, and she claws the man's face. I come to and look around, seeing more and more demons being escorted about and a man bleeding from his face.

"No, no," the man in the suit says, "Now I want to see what happens, what you will do."

She stands there ready to kill, arm up. "Prime behavioral experiment right here."

⊶ ⊙ ⊷

She starts looking around, confused, twitching her head back and forth trying to understand what this place is. I look at the man trying to stand back up on his feet. One of the male demons walks up to her and says, "We lost, just accept it."

She mutters something to him, "You disgust me, you traitor! You should get your wings torn off!"

He spits at her feet while he's pulled away. "We're just expendable anyways, just bastard sons and daughters."

A soldier grabs one of her horns and smashes her face into his knee while another man pulls on her other horn, holding her still as the blood drains from her nose.

"You have quite the kick and ferocity," the suited man tells her, pushing one of the soldiers away. She thrashes around but is held still as more and more men hold her down. Another man comes up behind and puts me into a hold, scraping my skin up from his body armor.

"I assume you'd like to leave now," the suited man tells Martta, "I'm sure you're thinking you've endured enough—"

"I'm fantasizing about tearing your throat out, actually," she replies. He flicks his hand in signal and two men start pulling her horns apart. She starts screaming in agony.

"Another experiment now, I'd like to see what's going to happen next."

The horn gives an unsettling *POP*, and the horn breaks off. She screams bloody murder, writhing on the floor. I scream and try to go to her, but am held back by the men. I look around to all the other demons averting their eyes.

They pull her back up, and she kicks the suited man full force, knocking him back. "You witch," he says, coughing. A dart flies into her neck and slowly calms down into unconsciousness, but manages to break free from the hold, falling to the floor.

"What are you going to do to her?"

"That is," he pauses, coughing, "classified."

Cold metal wraps around my wrist, and I start getting dragged off somewhere, my vision going dark. "You've made a lot of ruckus, Ostin," he says.

⧏⊙⧐

I was kept in isolation for days, with only the occasional visit from armed men to bring me food. I grew oddly lonely without Martta; even missing her. It was like my first visit here so long time ago.

The door opens, and a suited man walks through. "Hello Ostin," he says, "Take a look at this."

He hands me a tablet with a video feed; it takes me a moment, but I recognize Martta, cuffed multiple times at the arms and legs, writhing around on the ground. "She's been refusing food, and obviously is very violent."

"Why are you showing me this?" I ask. He places the tablet on the table.

"You did manage to get a substantial amount of information for us," he tells me, "We want more information about their homeworld. I'll let you in there with her."

"Or what?" I reply. Fear washes over me as he leans forward on the table."

"*Or* you'll go to federal prison for the rest of your life for treason," he states.

Two soldiers march in, pull me up by my arms and start marching me back out. After a few minutes of struggling, they toss me into Martta's room, but she doesn't acknowledge me. I look around to see a bed with blood on one side, and a single chair opposite the wall.

The door closes and she starts banging her head against the door, with one horn less on her head. "Martta, what are you doing?" I ask, "They're just going to put you in worse restraints."

She suddenly stops at my words. "What'd they send you in for?" she asks, sitting up against the wall, revealing all the dried blood from her wound.

"They want me to get more—"

"More what?" she seems oddly tranquil.

"They want to know about your home?" I tell her, "What it's like over there."

"Well, they'll have to kill me first," she says, standing up then smashing her restraints on the door.

"How long have you been doing this?" I ask.

"Not long enough," she replies striking the door again. I sit there and watch as she tries to compose herself after each swing.

"Are you okay?" I break my silence.

"I don't need *your* sympathy—"

I interrupt her, "We all need some emotional support."

"But I don't need yours," she whispers, falling down to the corner.

"Tell me about your home," I ask.

"Did they tell you to ask me that?"

I refuse to lie, "Yes, they did. But I'd still like to know."

"It's not like here," she tells, "There's not fake stone, or hardened air, or *machines*. There are trees and *bato* everywhere, fields of food."

"What color is your sky?" I continue.

"You'd call it green, but it often changes to red when the suns align on the horizon." she rests her head on the wall, and tears of blood flow down her cheeks, "We see things differently."

"You don't have electricity or anything?" I ask, "Must be pretty dull. How's your head?"

"What'd you expect?" she turns her head, revealing the massive open wound of blood and broken bone, "I just need all this to end."

"What about Kiira? Is she your sister?" I say, thinking about the other demon.

"No, she's a warrior like me, we just happen to get along enough to be friends."

Silence reigns as I can't think of anything else to ask. Finally, Martta breaks the silence, "They run out of questions?"

"I'm actually genuinely interested in your world," I say, "It's not every day I get to be imprisoned with an alien." I look to see Martta dozing off, probably from exhaustion. With no one to talk to, I do the same.

⊰⊙⊱

I naturally wake up lying on the floor. Panicked, I look around for Martta, but she's nowhere to be found. My eyes are drawn to the horn on the ground in front of me. The part that was attached to her skull had been sawed off, and inscriptions in her language had been carved all over the horn in glowing red.

Then I realize the handcuffs had been removed, and I was alone, locked in this room. I rush to the door and begin to slam my fist into it, shouting, "Let me out! Where is she?!"

After a minute or so, the door opens. That suited man greets me, and he commands that I walk with him. I reluctantly follow, and we walk in silence down halls and around corners. There are so many doors.

He stops and waves his hand in front of a door, and the locks begin to move. "I personally have been an advocate for this conflict to end. It was unanimous amongst all the demons that they are released back through a one-way portal."

The door opens and I see Martta sitting down, chained to a metal table. She is unresponsive.

"One way?" I ask.

The suited man nods. "You have two choices: You can join the military under a new name where we can keep an eye on you. Or we can send you to federal prison.

"But right now, as a courtesy, you can say goodbye."

He motions and lets me go inside the room. She looks up at me as some blood flows down her face.

"I heard they're letting you all back home."

She scoffs and twists her head, "All of them except me."

The suited man speaks through the intercom. "She, among some others, are being kept for experimentation. She's a young and prime specimen."

I look down sadly. "I'm sorry, but there's nothing I can do."

"You all deserve to burn in fire pits and drown in the grand sea," she says, avoiding me.

"Times up," the suited man says, opening back the door. Martta spreads her wings and lunges to the door, grabbing me and breaking the chains, pulling me with her through the door.

⬅ ⊙ ➡

She pulls me along as she rushes past the soldiers, snatching one of their guns. She dashes down the halls with me trailing behind her as she jumps and kicks people down.

She leads me through the hallways as if she knew the map of this place. We come to an elevator, and the access stairs to the side. Her wings spread wide, and she glides into the door to the access.

A loud crash and the doors burst open. Martta moves her wings to fly up and around the steps, leaving me to climb them the old fashioned way. But I try to run up as fast as I can.

"Hurry!" she shouts as I begin to slow down from exhaustion.

A soldier bursts through the next set of access doors. I freeze in fear, but he is quickly dispatched by the gun Martta holds. "Run!" she shouts to me again, bringing me out of my frozen state.

I begin again to run up the unrelenting steps upward to the next floor. They seem never-ending. And another set of access doors burst open with soldiers running through right behind Martta above me. Gunfire occurs and some of the men fall down the steps with one of them falling right by me.

Thinking quickly, I grab a grenade off one of the men's vests and continue to run. Martta kicks open one of the doors in front of her, calling out to me and firing her weapon.

A few moments later, I catch up to her, stopped by the sight of a brigade of soldiers with guns aimed at us. I promptly show them the grenade I stole from that fallen soldier, pulling the pin without letting go of the lever. I hold it in front of me.

They all freeze, and my hands shake. "Let them pass," the man that Martta had slashed in the face commands them.

All step to the side and Martta tugs on my arm, pulling me along. I see the infuriating look of that suited man, glaring at the two of us covered in gauze pads and medical tape. Martta doesn't even acknowledge him, as we dash past him.

She tugs my arm again, as she sharply turns right. I look at her firing the gun at glass doors. The bullet spider-webs the glass, but it doesn't break.

"Oh," the suited man walks over to us, "Please, let me."

He waves his hand, and the doors open. Very suspicious, indeed. Martta whirls around and fires a bullet into his leg as she runs into an open area.

The Portal to Hell. I was told that this portal was actually opened as a public event in an open field for people to watch. But after the first soldiers went in, they were met with a threat. This is when the military came in and build this entire facility around it. The center is this portal, with a protective metal mesh above us for containment.

I trip over a wire, and fall fantastically, releasing the grenade. This is how I'm going to die, tripping over an electrical wire and dropping a grenade.

The grenade explodes in a flash of light, and fog is spread everywhere. The sunlight fades away, and everything around me is covered by smoke.

"Come on!" Martta pulls me up, pulling me along. We run, hearing the steps of more soldiers marching in. I could imagine people were already in formation around here for protection.

The portal comes into view, and I peer through it, seeing that the smoke fills the view on the other side as well. But everything was as Martta told me, a green sky and trees everywhere.

"Shut it down!" a man cries out.

Martta turns around and embraces me. "Thank you for being different," she whispers to me, before strangely kissing me, "Do *not* follow me."

She pushes her torn-off horn into my hand, and leaves me, shoving me to the ground. Bullets fly through the smoke cloud, and an unsettling crackling of electricity emanate from the portal, as I see the image from the other side altering. But Martta makes it through.

The portal collapses from its cubic supports in a flash of light and a gust of wind. The smoke is blown away, revealing the soldiers closing in around me.

"Halt!" a man shouts, and I look in despair at a single metal wire reaching from the ground, broken off in the center of the cube.

A soldier walks up to me, pushing me over to my stomach, and placing handcuffs around my wrists. I look up to the other suited man with a disappointed look glaring at me.

"Your freedom was so close, Ostin," the suited man says, pinching his fingers together, "This close. And now, you're ours."

As the suited man said to me earlier, I was pronounced dead and given a new name. I was forced into a military division where I had a very close watch on me at all times. I was always suspicious of the people around from that point onward. They organized a funeral for me, which my father didn't even bother to attend. I was never allowed to contact him from that point on, but I didn't want to communicate with him anyways.

They used a tether to reopen the portal, and it was publicly announced that all remaining demons were going to be given a peaceful opportunity to go back through the portal, permanently, before it was officially closed. I was also allowed to keep Martta's horn. The inscriptions eventually lost their red glow, but I always kept it around me.

The only thing I knew for certain was that it was going to be a very, very long time until I was going to see Martta again.

Birth Of The Dragon King

⸸ ◎ ⸸

I RUSH THROUGH the streets, pushing and shoving people as I run to-ward the fire. I can see the blazes above the rooftops, set by the local triads. I run right past the casino I visited last night.

"You're one day is up, Li!" one of the workers shout at me as I run.

I make my way out near the rice fields to see my home up in flames, burning in a fervent fire. "Fu!" I cry out, running past those actively casting flames on my home.

One of them grabs my garments and it tears away as I burst through the flaming door. The heat is intense, but I search for my wife and daughter. Room after room, I feel my flesh beginning to char until I find them: my dear daughter burned to ash, wrapped by my wife's blackened body. I look around them to see focused burn marks all over the floor and walls.

I fall to my knees; wailing, not knowing what the purpose of is life is anymore. I hear something whispered into my ears, I turn to see no one, just my house falling down around me.

"Repeat it!" I hear a voice.

"Who are you?" I cry out, as a stream of flames glides through the air, like a serpent, into my nostrils. More streams of fire from all around fill my lungs; it feels comfortably warm. Eventually, the fire subsides, leaving a charcoal structure and two corpses.

I look down at my hands to see small flames dancing around my skin like the end of a candlestick. I overhear one of the men outside say, "Do you think he's still alive?"

"You think that what we should be worrying about—" another shouts, "No one told us he's a sorcerer!"

I make my way outside to see the three men standing there conversing.

"Li, you were given until sunrise, it's nothing personal—" he says, before I walk up and grab him by his garments.

"You killed!" I yell in his face. Something inside me awakens, and he bursts into flames. I let go of him as he flails around in pain until he falls dead.

"Now you've done it Li," another ruffian kicks me down. I prop myself up as he casts fire on me from his fists. I feel the warmth, but I'm not burned. I see the ruffian's foot coming for my face right before I blackout.

◄╟ ⊙ ╢►

"Xin Li," I hear our King speaking to me, "You've murdered Zhang Wong, and you are to be cast out to die in the wilderness."

"They killed my wife!" I call out, struggling to escape the heavy chain. I wail, breathing a flame from my mouth.

"Wong killed your wife and child," the King speaks, "He has paid in full. You are now going to be stripped of your magic."

He signals one of his magicians to come up to me. I breathe the flames at him, but he simply redirects them. He places his palm on my chest, and I feel the soul briefly knocked from my body. He pulls my essence away from me, like strings connected to every bit of my flesh, until something tears away.

"Now cast him out to the north, and leave him to die!"

I try to breathe fire, but nothing comes from my mouth. They chain me down even further to drag me into a barred carriage. As they close the carriage doors, I shout, "I'll be back to kill you."

"I look forward to it," the King replies.

◄◄ ⊙ ►►

After days of traveling in the cold snow, they finally throw me out of the carriage. They release the chains and kick me into the icy soil. "Now die out here, fire mage," one of them tells me.

I'm too weak to stand, but I roll onto my back in time to see the horses trotting into the distance. I eventually fell asleep from exhaustion, but when I woke I wandered for food.

The winter berries are bitter, but they've given me enough strength to walk. I try again to summon fire, but nothing. I look down at my hands, the tips of my fingers already blackened from the cold.

Something in the sky catches my eye. A long sky beast writhes around in the sky until crashing down to earth a day's journey up into the mountain from me. My mouth waters and my stomach churns at the thought of meat.

"What more can happen to me?" I ask myself, marching on for the beast. The sun rises to noon and sleeps in the evening, but I've arrived. The dragon is magnificent; striking iridescent blue and red scales, with white hair around its face. It's still breathing, but it labors. I look around at its wounded body. Chunks missing from cannon shots, others pinchushioned by crossbow bolts.

"C-come close," I hear it say

Unyielding, I walk to its face. "I haven't much more time, but I can give you what you seek."

"What is it that I seek," I retort back to the dragon.

"Revenge, spite," it replies, "I'll offer you a deal: take my soul upon you and you will be endowed with my power—"

"I'll do it," I jump on the opportunity.

It coughs, a terrible heaving sound, and I feel something pierce my chest like a dagger. When I look down, I see one of its teeth in my chest. The tooth is covered in strange patterns and inscriptions in some infernal language, seemingly burned into the item. "What did you do?" I utter, before falling to the ground. The world starts spinning before going dark.

⫷ ⊙ ⫸

My eyes shoot open and I gasp for air, being greeted by flames all around me, my lungs burning from the hot air. I sit up and look around to see a group of hunters trying to cremate me; they all look at me, scared.

"The demon!" one of them shouts, shooting a crossbow bolt, striking me in my shoulder. I shout in pain, but it snaps me out of my shock as I reflexively yank the bolt out. I feel for the gaping hole in my chest, where there the dragon's tooth should be, but it appears to be healed.

"Get him out of the fire!" I hear another one of the hunters shout. I look around to see the fire still ablaze, but I cannot feel the heat anymore. I stand and walk out of the fire, my bare feet brushing casually against the coals.

The world becomes clearer than it has ever been; colors are more vibrant. My muscles feel stronger too, not weary like they used to be. I look down at my chest and see a fantastic tattoo, similar to the dragon's scales spreading across my entire torso.

"Demon!" the man with the crossbow says again, firing at me again, but missing.

"Stop that," I raise my hand up. My arm begins to move by itself, extinguishing the flames right before my eyes. The deep ringing of a bell brings me to a foreign landscape.

I look around to see a misty haze covering everything below this mountain I'm atop. I look at my feet to see a small plateau.

"Welcome, Li," I hear a voice. I turn around to see a small, finely crafted tea table with some cups and a steaming pot. But shockingly, the Dragon is posing with its head at the table, its body extending out into the misty haze. I blink only for the dragon to vanish and a man appear, sitting at the table.

"Welcome? Where am I?" I ask the man, confused, "I'm not dead, am I?'

"No," he laughs, "You are not dead."

He appears to be wearing fine silk and gold, well-groomed and drinking some tea. "You've become my vessel, and I, your avarice for revenge. I am Yohan the heretic, dragon of the north."

I sit down to enjoy some tea with him on this exquisite landscape but find the tea to be missing from my cup. "What have you bestowed upon me as part of our deal?" I ask.

He smiles, "I've granted you the power of the mighty dragon: fire, and great strength."

"I see," I set the cup down, "Then what shall I do?"

He sets down his tea, his cup filled to the brim. "Kill the King, and become king yourself, perhaps?"

I smile back at him in a cold-hearted contract, and find I've been standing still amongst the hunters. "You've become an annoyance to me," I tell the troop of hunters as I use my new abilities to set them ablaze.

⊷ ⊙ ⊶

I look around, strangely filled with joy at the sight of the burning corpses of the hunters and the dragon, on Yohan's request. The smell of smoke is pleasant, especially the smoke of burning an enemy you know you've defeated.

I walk over to the tree that fell to the campfire the hunters had created, resting my hands on the broken fibers of wood until it begins to blaze. As it burns, I feel warmth in my chest, like an animal chasing its prey.

The fire dances around like a rabbit, bouncing to each branch, tree, and shrub alike. I walk through the fire, all the way down the mountain until I reach the kingdom's walls. Before long, the entire forest is afire. I bathe in its warmth, anticipating the predator catching its food.

The path clears enough for me to see the city setting off signals to alert the people of the fire. I scream out, breathing out a great blue flame in response.

Eventually, I arrive at the base of the mountain, seeing their army digging a trench and setting up a fire barrier. One of them notices me walking out of the burning forest. He alerts the others and slowly they try to cross the trench to rescue me.

"Come down into the trench!" he foolishly commands, not knowing who I am. I begin to run, preparing to jump over the trench. He looks bewildered as I soar above him, but I crash into the barrier and all the other people start pulling me over.

They finally manage to pull me across the barrier and I fall to the ground. I look up to be face to face with one of the triads who banished me into the wilderness.

"Fate is a cruel thing, Li," he says, expelling fire from his fist directed at my face. I breathe in, consuming the fire as it comes.

"Impossible," the gangster whispers under his breath, "Enough with the tricks!" He thrusts his hand into the dirt and extracts the metal around his fists.

"No tricks," I reply, "only revenge!" I expel the fire back from my lungs, burning him to his bones. He falls back as I rise to my feet, flailing his body in pain until he suddenly stops. The others stare at me in horror; looking at my uninjured body walking back towards the city.

◄◄ ⊙ ►►

I look up at the great palace of our King; fine paint, golden statues; the best one can afford. I stand before the closed gate to the enormous courtyard.

"Who goes there!?" a guard shouts from behind the gate, "Speak now or be struck down!"

I hear Yohan the dragon whisper into my ears. "You shall be the new King of this land, state it so," he says.

I repeat, "I am the new King of this land, allow me into my palace!" The guards begin to laugh and one of them manages to tell me to leave.

"Grant me strength, Yohan," I whisper. Energy flows throughout my body into one of my hands as the image of a cup is filled with a few drops of tea; I grab a portion of the gate and begin to lift. I throw all the strength I have into it, and the gate begins to rise.

"Hey!" a guard shouts thrusting his spear through the gate. I dodge the sharpened point by a hair and break it off with my spare hand. As soon as I'm through the gate, I drop it and it slams into the ground with the warrior underneath.

More warriors swarm around me, thinking they might have a chance against the dragon inside me. I feel warmth inside my chest, burning and dancing around in my lungs. The fire begins to expel out, coating the ground and burning the soldiers. Even still they try to attack.

One after another, I dispel them with my overwhelming strength, making my way to the palace. Their words cannot pierce me, nor can their spears.

⊶⊙⊷

I punch the palace door one last time, breaking through the brace they had put up. "I'm here, my King!" I yell out, "I've come!"

The door swings open, revealing the coward sitting on his throne. His two kingsguard ready their weapons ready to defend him with their very lives.

"You've sold your soul," he says, "Haven't you, Li?"

I point my finger at him. "You sold yours a long time ago, didn't you?"

"I've made my choices," he replies, "Now you make yours."

I march up and dispose of the kingsguard, one after another. As I march on his footsteps, breathing fire all around. Through the flames, he just sits there, unharmed. I reach my hand around his throat and lift him up off his chair.

"I'll be taking your throne for myself," I whisper in his dying ear. Nothing but his gasping for life makes it to my ears. I tighten my grip until his body grows lifeless. I feel a great spirit leave this presence.

I toss the former king aside and sit down on my new throne, thinking of what I should command this country next: conquest is fitting for me, I think. More warriors and soldiers come marching in, not expecting their new King.

"Go on," I taunt them, "Go ahead and try."

I see one of the military leaders stand there, staring at me. Suddenly, he drops to one knee, followed by the people standing behind him.

⊶⊙⊷

Colors

"THE PRETTIER you are, the faster they sell," my manager tells me, tossing a scarf in my direction. My stylist catches it and continues to dress me right before I get on stage.

"It could be a blue dipped canvas, Charlie, as long as my name is on it, it'll sell no problem!" I shoot back.

"Breathe," my stylist commands, checking my breath. They keep telling me the audience can smell my breath from twenty feet away, but it's all rumor.

I hear the audience applauding for me, and my manager starts pushing my shoulders through the curtain. "And here he is!" the announcer calls me out, "Filip Rowe, extraordinary painter; sculptor of the canvas."

I bow a little as part of an onstage routine. "*Bonjour* everyone, welcome Jamie!"

"Now, please, Filip, tell us the story of this beauty," she gestures to the painting by her side, but it's tilted towards the light, obscuring my view of which one it is.

"So, if I recall correctly," I clear my voice, "I woke up one morning, in my hotel in Venice, and these beautiful clouds in the shape of a woman literally smiling back at me from the sky. And I knew just then, I had to put it on canvas."

I wink at Jamie, whose name I nearly forgot just now. "That's amazing *and beautiful*, Filip," she says, winking back, "You must really have an eye for color. Bu-uh-t, we're not here to flirt, we're here to sell."

She pulls out a notepad and starts scanning the pages with her striking blue eyes. "According to my notes here, we're starting at one million Euros flat. Anyone for one million flat?" I smile and show some teeth when the crowd begins to boost up the price one by one. This is my favorite part of my job.

⊶⦿⊷

I pull my fur mittens out of my bag and slide them over my ice-cold hands to protect them from the cold wind today. *It's so frickin' cold today,* I think to myself, *I thought spring had come.*

I toss my scarf around my neck and button up the top button on my shirt. As I walk, I pass by a beggar on the side of the road. "Can you spare any money?" he begs.

"I built my own bank account by painting, one after another," I tell him, "No reason why you can't do the same." I promptly turn my back and go on my way.

Later down the road, I wave for a nearby taxi. A woman runs up, yelling, "Excuse me!" I wave my hand more to beckon the cab. "Excuse me, Mr. Filip!" she comes up to me, "Can you answer a few questions?"

My mind occupies itself with thoughts of the cab coming, but I still say, "Yes, yes of course. But you have until a cab comes."

She sits there, wasting the time I've given her by rummaging through her purse, finally pulling out a tape recorder. "What painting did you recently sell?" she asks, pressing record on the device.

"The woman in the sky."

A newspaper flies by in the wind and lands smack on her face, knocking her glasses away. She pulls the paper off to reveal her striking green eyes, complemented by her wonderfully red lipstick.

"My bad, sorry," she says, "In there, the woman said you have quite the eye for color; do you think *it* will ever happen to you?"

My mind focuses on her annoying little words. "I don't have time to believe in voodoo nonsense; my cab's here."

The cab pulls up and I rush to get inside away from the journalist. I set my bag beside me in the seat, and say to the driver, "Let me tell you, I hate journalism."

"Me too, where're you headed?" the driver replies.

"1024 Broddock Street."

I hear him start to chuckle, "Oh, We have a rich fellow in my cab today. Where you from, you're not from here?"

"I'm from Chicago, actually."

"Never heard of it," he laughs.

I pull out my sketch pad and begin to draw the journalist. After the rough sketch, I pull out the red marker to fill in her lips, though it's not the same red, just not right.

"We're here, rich man," the driver tells me, "Be sure to leave me a nice tip, Chicago man."

I retrieve my wallet from the bag and hand him a couple of bills for the ride. "Keep the change," I tell him. I step right out of the cab and take a gander at the beautiful estate I own here, or at least am leasing, in this beautiful city.

⊣⊢ ⊙ ⊢⊣

I sit back at my small table for two and pour some fine wine into a glass. I start skimming through the phone book for any Jamies as I'm pretty sure she's fallen for my immense charm; but there are so many Jamies in this area: Kelly, Badiola, Coleiro, etc. The list keeps on going.

I take a nice swig of my *Grand Cru* and stare at the list one last time, trying to remember the name of the company hosting the auction the other night. I suppose I choose eenie, meenie, minie, moe.

I reach out to my house phone that's just barely within my grasp and start dialing. The phone starts to ring and I whisper to myself, "I hate this."

"Bonjour," I hear a man on the other side. I stand up and walk over to the anchor and pull down to hang up.

"No-uh-t who I was expecting," I say, starting to dial the next number.

"Bonjour?" I hear a woman greet me.

"Hi, I'm calling about the art show the other night?" I reply.

"I'm sorry, I think you have the wrong number—" I hang up.

"Ugh," I sigh, dialing yet another number, "I'm calling for Jamie? From the art show?"

The phone promptly hangs up, but then begins to ring from an incoming call. I put the phone down and pick it back up. "Hello?"

"Calling for Filip Rowe?" a familiar female voice says.

"Filip speaking," I reply, "I was actually filing through a phone book for you; funny thing, right?" I begin to awkwardly chuckle.

◂┼ ⊙ ┼▸

Coffee in Paris with a beautiful woman, what's better than that for the life of a bachelor. The wind blows about the litter and trash scattered about the location and ruffles my silk scarf. So many homeless oddly enough hang out around this establishment, but she insisted that this was the best coffee and pastry: the Ancheta Café.

"Bonjour, *cher*," she greets me, "How are you doing today? Better now that I'm here, I'm sure."

"Can't say it's any worse," I smile, "But life is going great."

A large brown man comes and prances out of the doors and rushes to our tableside. "The first date?" he smiles.

"I guess—" I try to reply before being cut off from him.

"Ah-ha!" he laughs quite loudly, "I know exactly what you want!" he goes and happily prances off back inside to presumably to get us our coffee.

She leans over and presses her lips against mine, leaving a faint taste of cherry lipstick. As she leans back, I think to myself, *sublime kissing skills.*

"Who's home would you rather go to?" she asks.

"Mine, for sure, but I want my pastries first, and the coffee."

◁‖⊙‖▷

I sit up at the side of the bed and outstretch my back, popping all the bones into place; I swing my arms around and look at the beautiful woman in the bed next to me. *I'm still young,* I think to myself.

I stand up and start walking to the kitchen to get some wine. "Where are you going, love?" she inquires of me, pulling the sheets over herself.

I turn and smile. "I was going to get some wine and the newspaper."

"You still read that?" she asks.

"Newspaper is still a reliable news source, the television is too biased," I tell her.

I slip my feet into the slippers and make my way to the front of the house. I look out the window and see overcast skies. The door unlocks and I see today's paper laying right there at the base of the steps.

"Whatcha waiting for?" she asks, standing there in my dress shirt, "Back sore?"

"I'm not old, but out of shape," I say, picking up the paper and walking back inside.

She makes the coffee for this morning and hands me a cup of it. "Black and hot?" I ask.

"As black and hot as the instant coffee gets," she replies, "anything good in the paper today?"

"Yeah, there's a story about me," I explain, "There was a reporter the other day who interviewed me for a couple of minutes; must've gotten her story published."

I pick up the coffee and it splashes of my arm a little and burns me.

She pulls out a cigarette and pops it into her mouth. "There doesn't seem to be a whole lot of your own dialogue here, Filip."

"Yeah, she wasn't very proactive," I say.

She pulls out a lighter, "Do you have a smoking policy here?" she asks.

"Landlord doesn't mind," I reply, "You don't want any coffee?"

"No, it's bad for the stomach," she tells me.

I stare at the newspaper and actually read the story: Acclaimed artist, Filip Rowe, doesn't believe in the 'Voodoo; tunnel vision of love. "I don't believe in voodoo nonsense," he said, before storming off into a cab. Though many still lay in disbelief about this seemingly supernatural event, many have legitimate testimonials about its real-world impact.

"Can't say I believe in what she has to say," I tell Jamie.

⊩ ⊙ ⊪

Stroke after stroke, I create yet another masterpiece here under the sun in the Ancheta Café, but the pencil breaks underneath the nose, leaving an unwanted, but permanent mark.

"How's my portrait looking?" she asks, breaking her pose to take a bite of her toasted bread.

"Have you ever looked into a mirror, Jamie?" I ask back.

She laughs and goes back into her pose. I find a red marker sitting beside all my instruments of art and start on the lips. It's not the right color red, but beautiful and vibrant nonetheless. After the lips, I start on some faint color around the cheeks.

I look down at the piece and realize; *Crap!* I used green on the eyes, not Jamie's striking blue. I look around for any other mistakes and realize the jaw isn't right, the nose is wrong; I've been drawing the reporter from that while ago. I tear the page out and crumple it up.

"No good," I tell her.

"Hey!" she shouts, "What happened?"

My vision starts to tunnel and grow dark. "It happens all the time," I manage to say before falling out of my chair onto the ground.

Next thing I know, I'm lying there on the cold concrete floor of the Café with a makeshift pillow underneath my head and my feet propped on a chair; something else is off though, I can feel it.

"What-what just happened?" I ask aloud, hoping for someone out there to respond in my delusions.

"You just passed out, Filip," I hear Jamie say, sounding very angry, "It seems that I'm not the one for you."

I look around for her beautiful face, but I finally see what's happened; her face faded to shades of gray; the world to shades of gray.

Jamie rushes away, tossing my drawing of the other woman. "Are you alright, sir?" somebody snaps his fingers around my face, "You're lucky I was an ambulance worker off duty."

I fumble my way on my knees, the man helping me up. When I'm on my feet, I push him away. "No, no, I'm fine," I refuse his help but fall back down. *No, no, no, I am fine*, I think to myself.

⟨⟨ ⊙ ⟩⟩

I pull out another blank canvas, tossing the old one to the side. I make my strokes, but none of them are straight. I make a stroke for the eye, but the charcoal shatters and marks up the paper with smudges and stray marks. *Don't take this from me*, I pray. My hands have been stricken with tremors and it seems my eyesight grows worse as the weeks go by.

"Please, God, don't take this!" I shout, throwing the canvas aside.

I kneel down to grab the largest piece of broken charcoal and try my best to trace out a face on a fresh canvas. Slowly the face of the reporter emerges. I go along with it and begin to draw the finer details, but it's not what I want. I wipe my hands to shade the face, but the tremors in my hands come again and ruin the sketch.

Suddenly, the landline starts ringing louder than I would like it to right now, but I make my way over and answer the phone. "Hello, Fillip speaking," I say into it.

"Filip! It's Charlie," the phone replies with my manager on the other end.

"Hi, Charlie, what's up?"

"Nasty rumors are going around saying that you're going to stop painting," he tells me, "Heard you had a bad fainting spell at a coffee shop the other week."

"Yes, I did," I explain, "I hit my head pretty hard, just in the recovery process—"

"You can't paint anymore, or see color, can you?" he interrupts.

"I'm just in the recovery process—" the phone hangs up, and I'm left with the annoying ringing of the phone again.

⇇ ⊙ ⇉

"I'm diagnosing you with Monochromacy color-blindness and muscle tremors."

"I know that doctor," I say, "But can it be fixed?"

"I've seen this a few times, but those were all, so far anyway, permanent cases," she continues.

"I mean, this isn't magic right," I go on, "Stuff like this doesn't happen out of the blue."

"All the other cases of this did," she replies, "whether it's magic or genetics, I have no idea."

Damn this, I think to myself as she hands me some more prescriptions.

"Follow the exit signs, *carefully.* Take care, Filip."

I get up onto my weak legs and make my way down the hallways, hands on the walls. Down the hallway is the discharge lady with the paperwork. "Insurance card?" she asks.

I fish out my wallet and try to fumble the cards I need out, but just end up dropping the wallet on the counter. "Need help?" she asks.

"No, no," I persist, "I got this." But I don't have this; it takes several minutes to get all the cards out. With two of my fingers, I manage to pinch the cards and hand them to the lady, handing me the paperwork back.

Under the overbearing embarrassment from the other person waiting, I cover my face with my hand. I manage to vaguely sign the paper with scribbles and chicken scratches and push it back to the desk lady. "You know, I almost bought one of your paintings, many years ago when you first started." she tries to make the small talk, "Your skill has definitely gotten better over the years."

"I apparently won't be painting much anymore," I reply.

"That's a shame, you're really good at it," she says, "You're good to go."

⊷⊙⊶

I stare at the newspaper, written in French, a glass of fine wine in hand. The paper has it plastered all over that I'm leaving the art industry. Every time my hand twitches I spill a little on the paper.

KNOCK, KNOCK, I hear from the door. I set the glass down and wobble my way to the door on my weakened legs. I turn the knob and I'm greeted by Jamie.

"I-I left some clothes here," she says, averting her eyes from mine.

"Right, come on in," I invite her in, "I put them in the bags there."

"Thanks," she says, "You don't seem alright, Filip."

"I'm aware." everything is gray, everything even blurs together sometimes. I watch her as she grabs her bags and walks back up to the door.

"Heard you're going to stop painting," she tells me, "I wish you wouldn't."

"Haven't got many choices," I reply, seeing her out. She waves goodbye, and that's probably the last time I'm going to see her. As she leaves, I see on the door and eviction notice. So many emotions steamroll over my mind; if I don't have a place to live, I'll get deported back to America. Piece by piece, my life is falling apart.

⤃ ⊙ ⤀

Some officers break down my door and march up to me. They pick me up off my weakened legs. "Don't," I plead, "I have nowhere to go."

"Too bad, Mr." he replies.

"Where am I supposed to go?" I shout.

"The street," the man says, "You've been unable to complete your legal agreement living here."

"I have nowhere to go!" they toss me literally to the curb. I trip and fall to the ground, scraping both my knees. I kneel back up and start to tear up. "I have nowhere to go."

The officers slam the door shut and lock it. "You can't stay here anymore, you have to leave."

I try and stand, but I fall right back down. The world is gray and bland, but my life is black, in pieces. I look down at my hands on the soil and they begin blurring together into a mush of shades.

I attempt to stand once more and begin to wander towards the demise of my career, my life. This is oblivion for me: begging for the help of others. I eventually wander aimlessly into the bustling part of town, where the homeless live.

I'm pathetic; bringing myself down to the very thing that I hate. I rub my face, feeling the stubble that seems to have come back for good in a decade. Broken, I snatch a banknote, but let it ride the wind into oblivion, just as I am.

⁜

"Yup," someone says, waking me from a nap, "That's him."

Three officers approach me as I lift my head. I can barely recognize them as people at the moment. "Are you Filip Rowe?" they ask me.

"Yes," I barely mutter.

"You're being deported, Filip," one of them reminds me, "You've been unable to secure housing or work, you're being shipped back to America."

I struggle to sit up to properly face them as a man, and the burly one reaches out to help me on my feet, but I knock his hand away. Regardless of my apparent wishes, he grabs me and lifts me to my feet, followed by the cold steel of handcuffs.

I think back, trying to remember the world of colors, I think that the police vehicles were an ugly, but reminiscent yellow. They help me inside the back and we drive off as I try to think about the rainbows that used to be. That shopping center used to have a lovely shade of violet on the signage.

Before I know it, I'm face to face with immigration. "Name, birthday, birthplace for the record, Mr. Rowe," she says.

How I must've nearly forgotten. "Rowe, Filip; April first; Chicago, Illinois," I tell her.

"Do you remember your social security number as given to you by the United States Government?" she continues.

"No," I reply.

"Sign here," she commands, "For general acknowledgment of your current situation."

I raise my hands, filled with the tremors that have infected my entire body. She pulls out an ink sponge and instructs the officer to sign with my fingerprint. The officer rolls my finger on the sponge and on the paper, and that was it.

"Thank you," the desk woman says, but I'm herded off. They lead me into a room full of other gray masses assumed to be other homeless.

"Please, I beg," trying to turn back, but they resist and set me down into a seat. "I don't belong here with them!" I shout as they leave.

"We're not all that bad," someone says, "Where're you going?"

I try to ignore him, but the gray mass persists. "Just trying to make conversation here, it'll be awhile. But I know when no one is interested, *Filip.*"

Crap, I think to myself, *They all know who I am now.* I now have to be lumped in with these lowlifes. I continue to hear chuckles and snickers throughout my extended wait inside this asylum.

⏮ ⊙ ⏭

Damn Chicago, there's a reason why I left you, I say to myself. No place for someone like me; it's too damn cold here. The days begin to blend together too, just like the gray masses when they come; are they buildings or are they people, who am I to know?

I think it's been a year and a half wander from corner to corner, sometimes being able to see where I'm going or not. On occasion, I find a nice warm spot to settle, before being kicked, away of course.

I can barely distinguish between the sky and the horizon anymore. My hearing has impaired as well over time, so all the city chatter has become muffled; but clear as day, like the Swiss rivers into my ear canal, I hear music. The sweet, wonderful sound of a woman singing. I can't help but begin flowing down in tears at the sound: so heavenly.

I must've lost myself in bliss; before I knew it, it's gone. I open my eyes for the last time before the night to get some sunlight, and things seem to be a little more distinguished. Gone so quickly, a brief taste of something I took for granted. *How I wish for it back,* I think to myself.

⊰⊙⊱

The wonderful music plays about every week or so, so I try to stick around the area. Every time it plays, I hear that woman sing and it's so incredible. I don't quite remember what day it is, but the sweet, sweet music marks the beginning of the week for me.

When the music stops, I feel like I can see better with the occasional flash of color; O', how I miss it, the vibrancy is sublime.

I look up to see what must be the trickery of my senile mind, but I think I see a woman walk past me clear as day. Bright red scarf blowing in the wind as a lady's lips, while her hair flowing back and forth. Before I know it, she's gone too.

"Gone so quickly," I whisper, "But oh how beautiful."

The day goes by, swamps of dreary gray followed by the darkening of the world and the brightening in the morning. Again and again, until the day of music arrives. The smooth notes of the saxophone, the slow ringing of the high hats, and best of all, the angelic vocals of this mystery woman.

⊪ ⊙ ⊫

SNAP! SNAP! I hear someone's fingers go. A blurry hand moves back and forth, followed by a muffled speech that I can't quite make out. *Who is this?* I ask myself.

I feel something dropped into my lap and I run my fingers of the plastic bag, filled with mystery items. Condensation already is forming on the surface in this frigid weather.

The day turns to night, and I'm greeted by that music from around the corner. The smell of coffee is becoming more apparent to me along with a new clarinet player, but beautiful music all the same. And that wondrous woman and her voice; I could listen to her forever. Her voice paints itself into my mind with all the colors that I think used to be.

The music stops after a while, and I prepare to wait the required week to hear it again.

"Hey!" I make out from the crowd. It seems to be a woman, "Hey you!"

SNAP! SNAP! My eyes shoot open, with the entire world in all its clarity burning itself into my retinas. Anxiety fills my chest and I forget where I am, looking around at all these things around me in the sharpness of black and white.

"Screw it," she says, walking off, "You're just like another homeless man."

Wait! I call out in my head, *Where are you going?!*

A car horn walks as it drives past me, the pitch going up and down as it speeds away. The lights are too bright, all the mysterious figures rushing past. It's so entirely overwhelming; everything I've missed, most of it coming back to me. Everything, but the color.

⪡ ⊙ ⪢

I stare myself down in this disgusting gas station mirror. The stench is almost overpowering, almost unbearable. It took an entire night before I could take in all the world again, it was all too much. *Perhaps my sense of smell should've been taken*, I think to myself.

My sight and my hearing come and go as they please, sometimes on the whim of a heartbeat. The bag I was given were much-needed toiletries, including the razor I've been scraping my face with. I rub my hands up and down my face, feeling the patchy, but rough shave job from my trembling hands.

I go to shave more hair off my face, but fumble too much and drop the razor in the God-forsaken sink. *Damn*, I think to myself. I reach down and rinse it off with the questionable water.

A few minutes later, there's no more beard; just short stubble. I toss the chipped razor into the trash and make my way outside. The sun beats down on my skin just as the cold wind brushes past my naked face.

I scavenge my pockets for some fragrance and start walking over to the coffee shop where the woman sings tonight. My legs are still wary, but I've been able to walk fairly well ever since that event a few days ago. My trip to the coffee shop buffers on and off as disorientation strikes me so often. There's ringing in my ears as well sometimes.

The sun begins to set on my gray world as the coffee shop is in sight. The woman begins to sing once more, illuminating the walkway through the concrete jungle to her stage in flowing raindrop of reds and yellows and rivers of blues. I'm so mesmerized by the sight of what I see now when she sings.

One step after another in a parade of pinks and purples, she is there. That reporter from all that time ago; she's the one after all this time, how could I not have seen it? I take a seat and let myself experience this is in all its glory, and she's at the center of it all. She must've given up reporting, and moved on to a different kind of art.

I could listen to her forever.

December 19, 2099

❖

DECEMBER 19TH, YEAR 2099: The day that changed everything for humanity. That cold, icy Saturday morning in the tundra of northern Greenland, two corpses were dug up under a tent beneath the snow, a mother and a newborn baby. Mother had died from shock and hypothermia from childbirth. The more interesting of the corpses was that of the baby; it seemed to have been alive for multiple days showing signs of struggle and eventually dying of starvation. The child's blood-alcohol content was enough to keep the blood from freezing. What was guessed to be the father was found about a mile from the site, who died from hypothermia and was scavenged by wolves or something. Later analyses of the newborn found that he was born with something very unusual: a unique 25th chromosome.

About two weeks later in the same tundra, another newborn was found by researchers in the area studying a local native tribe. The child was nicknamed Olaf by one of the researchers due to his ability to survive extremely cold temperatures. They took the child to a research facility to study him. DNA testing found another 25th chromosome that allowed him to withstand temperatures in excess of -2° and 180° Fahrenheit before showing signs of tissue damage.

Everything went downhill since then, with the number of mutant births growing every year. I started as a detective back in '97 and moved to a special department to investigate mysterious deaths that could be connected to these new people with the 25th chromosome. By 2105, most of these births were in the eastern parts of Canada and the US, but

Some happened as far west as Kansas and as south as North Carolina. By 2110 these births started occurring in all of North America, Western Europe, and Parts of Eastern Asia with the US accounting for a third of all those births.

The year 2116 marked the official when these births occurred on every continent except Antarctica. By this time, there were cartels and gangs utilizing the now teenagers with 25 chromosomes throughout the entire world. Crimes became more gruesome, and my job became a helluva lot more interesting. The science guys in the labs had to create an official classification system for these abilities, and much of the civilized world was forced to have each person with 25 registered and accounted for, even if they didn't express supernatural abilities, going as far as testing the fetus as soon as possible. Governments took a lot of heat for that, but it made the world a safer place, just not an equal one.

It's been a smidge more than twenty-six years since I started my police work and seeing what these adults with 25 have to go through, you'd think it was racist 1960's you learned about in school. Some of the kids are working and living normal lives, while others do more exotic work. Some of these kids aren't, and they turn to crime where they're exploited for being able to breathe fire or of the sorts.

For me at this point, I'd like to say I've seen it all and that it's just the daily grind all of us have to go through at this point.

◀◀ ⊙ ▶▶

"Pretty classic F2 scene," one of the lab guys tells, "You got a light?"

I pull out a pack of cigarettes and pass one to him with my lighter.

"You're still carrying around this old zippo? Hasn't run out of gas yet?" he asks me. I pull one out of the box and light it in my mouth.

"No, I had to refuel it a couple of weeks ago. Can you identify the bodies?"

"Can't tell for sure without running lab tests, but the pile of ashes over by the door has metal teeth and gems matching the description of the guy you were looking for."

"What about the other two?" I inquire.

"We'll have to check dental records, all the blood was burned."

I walk over to the side of the building where the wall had been blown out. The F2 must've hit a gas pipe and caused a small explosion. The body in the corner away from the other two seems to be the enforcer for the drug dealer we were looking for, too.

"Damn, I could've gotten some good leads from him," I say to myself.

Someone walks up behind me; another detective from this area. "You think you know what happened?"

"Not too sure, but it looks like Jacob Keens over here was burning someone for that LSD dealer over in the corner and let it get out of control. This hole right here is probably from a gas line that got too hot.

"Alright, let's start bagging bodies and get in the cleaning crew!" the detective shouts to everyone, "Hey, I'm sorry to hear about your partner."

"Eh, the service was good, but it's an occupational hazard," I reply.

"Drive safe, detective, it's a little dangerous on these streets."

And that was that for the day, I get into the car and drive back to the department.

◄◄ ⊙ ►►

I repeatedly press the arrows on my keyboard moving through all the files on the screen. Sergeant comes barreling through the door and slaps a folder on my desk.

"What's this?" I inquire.

"The files for your new partner," he tells me, "You got twenty minutes to look over them."

I chuckle, "You must be busy today, last time I got thirty."

"That was twenty years ago," he chuckles back.

I start to flip through the pages; graduated 9th in his class, and has an associate's degree in forensics. Looks younger than he is, but he's impressive. Under Extra Notes, I find something new for the first time in a long time: has 25 chromosomes.

"He's got 25?"

"Yeah, the higher-ups picked him, and I had to assign him somewhere," he explains, "Figured a grizzled man like you could put a thick beard on this kid."

"Had to shave two times a week when I first started."

"Damn right," he says, "Be sure to not get lazy."

Sergeant walks back out, and I flip through this new kid's health records and stuff. Top fifteen on his physical scores, but scored just above the limit for the psych exam. More reading reveals that he's a non-expressing 25. Very interesting kid.

Sergeant knocks on the glass door for me to come outside to meet the new guy. I press the lock button on the computer and make my way out of my office.

"Detective, this is your new partner, Carter Zeemo," he tells me.

"Good to meet you, Carter," I reach out my hand, "Just finished reading your file.

"Impressed by what you read?" Carter asks.

"More than once, you have any real-world experience?" I return.

"No, sir. Fresh out of school."

"They give you your gun?"

Sergeant chimes in, "New guys don't get guns anymore, not after that one guy when berserk a few years back. He needs two weeks."

"I thought we solved that one."

"We did, but the state didn't like what happened regardless."

One of the guys walks a troubled teenager to the interrogation room in the background of the office rush. The intercom starts to spit static and someone starts to talk. "We have a suspect for detective Jameson's case in the back."

Sergeant slaps my shoulder. "You guys are up."

I slap Carter's shoulder and start making my way to the back. I look back to see him brushing his shoulder and following suit.

"Witnesses saw this kid running from the scene, and when we caught up to him, he said he could give info so he wouldn't serve time."

"I don't think that's how it works," I tell the officer.

"Well, one of the judges has a soft spot, right?"

I open the door to see a well built white kid with a lopsided buzz cut in a wife beater cuffed to the table. "What are you in for, kid?"

"I don't wanna serve no time, so I figure I could give you somethin'," he tries to say.

"I don't think that's how it works," I start to tell him, "How old are you?"

"Eighteen years young in a week."

"You got your ID in your wallet there?"

"Yessir," he confirms.

I reach for the burned leather wallet sitting on the table and open it up. A couple of 20s, a debit, and state ID with registration. I pull out the registration and look over it.

"So you're a RH4? Haven't seen a level four in here in a minute."

"I don' know what that means, sir."

I look to Carter, "Can you go get his criminal file?" He turns around and leaves.

"Resistance to heat, that's what RH means," I tell him.

He shakes his head up and down. "I can barely feel the red steel next to my hand."

"And you said you have info for us?"

"Yessir."

"Well, talk away, I have about an hour."

Carter walks back in with a thick manila folder and hands it to me. "This kid definitely has a record," He tells me.

"No kidding," I reply, opening the folder and start to scan the documents inside.

"That buildin' with the big hole in it a couple of days ago, I was in it when it went boom."

"Do you know who was in there when it 'went boom'," Carter asks.

"Yessir."

He starts to spill the beans and confirms that it was the LSD drug lord we were looking for, and he corroborates the lab results for Jacob Keens as the F2 enforcer we were tipped off about.

"Well, that is indeed useful information," I tell him.

"So that means I don't get jailed, right?"

"No—" Carter starts to give him the situation.

I interrupt my partner, "We can work out something with a judge, or something. Tell me, do you know your IQ?"

"86, sir, and mama's proud ovit."

"Well, if the judge is a nice one, you'll serve a low time and you'll get a real job when you get out."

"Dammit," the kid says, "That punk was lyin' to me."

"Who?" Carter asks.

"Well, I'm not gettin what I wanted now, so I'm not talkin."

"Yes—" Carter starts to raise his voice, but I stop him.

"Well, you gave us good stuff, but we have to move you to a cell and you'll see a judge pretty soon; I'll put in word for you though, you have a very useful skill."

The kid shakes his arms around only to find he's still cuffed to the table. "Carter, you mind filling out the paperwork?"

He glares at me, picks the files from the table and follows suit.

◄╫ ⊙ ╫►

"Jonathan Buckle, HR4," Amy starts reading off the kid's file, "You wanted to put in a good word for him?"

"Yes, ma'am. He was compliant with our interrogation and regardless of his," I pause to look through the multiple pages of his misdemeanors, "lengthy record, they're mostly petty theft 'cuz he's too stupid to go to school or do general work."

"Well, most of these teens you bring in are generally good people when they come out, so I'll trust you," the judge tells me, "The most it looks like I'll be able to do is maybe three fourths of his sentence."

"Well, I wouldn't expect much more considering his record."

"Hopefully he pays off; his kind is in high demand in grunt work."

"Thanks," I start packing my things, "I'm not going to take any more of your time."

"How's the honnies?" she laughs as she waves.

"I ain't got the time or the money," I chuckle back as I slip past the door.

"How much is she shaving off?" Carter asks me, popping off from leaning on the wall.

"She said three fourths on my better judgment."

"Well, how good is your judgment?"

"I'd give myself an eighty-five out of a hundred today," I reply, "Let's get going, there's something we have to investigate."

"What did you schedule?"

I move up my sleeve and check my watch. "We just have to talk around looking for new leads on this LSD bust."

"How long has it been going on?"

"I've been working on it for the past year, but we only started getting information two months ago. We were contacting Jacob Keens up until a week before he died."

"Any other contacts?" he asks.

"They all went under the radar after that incident."

"What are you planning then?"

"Most of them are underage 25s, so I've been trying to contact their family."

"How's that going?"

The front doors slide open and a gust of cold wind pushes through. "Terribly."

⇇ ⊙ ⇉

I puff my cigarette one last time and flick the burning butt into the gutter before we walk up to the door. This is the last known location of any of Jacob's relatives.

"Smoking's pretty bad for you, you know."

"I don't have time to quit," I tell Carter, knocking on the door.

"Thought it went out of style a hundred years ago."

"Maybe."

The door opens up revealing an older black man with badly shaped gray facial hair and a receding hairline. "Ah, damn. Whaddya cops want?"

Carter starts speaking before me, "We're looking for anyone who's had contact with a young man named Jacob Keens."

"Uh," the man mumbles, "I haven't seen that moron in a year."

"We're investigating his death and other related events," I explain, "Can you point us to anyone who might've had contact with him since you last have seen him?"

"There was this cracker with fake gold teeth who was hangin' out with him last I saw him; talking about mountains of money and drugs or somethin.'"

"Yeah, he's also one of the deaths we're investigating."

"Look, I got my dinner in the nuker," the man tells us while closing the door, "Don't come back."

"You'd think all these cameras everywhere would help with this."

"You'd think, but criminals find their way around. The city doesn't like us using them anyways."

"Who's next?" Carter asks me.

"We have an address for the mother of one of the ash piles."

"I was reading the files for this case, why don't we just raid the stockpiles, we know where they are."

"Their labs tend to be booby-trapped, and besides, we don't have the resources to fight kids who breathe fire."

"Don't we know where the ring leaders are?"

"Most of them aren't in the city. Gold mouth was an exception we were trying to snuff out."

We both get in the car and I shift it into gear. During the silent ride, I notice a couple of tweakers taking a nap in an alleyway. We make it to the address to find a typical, low-income apartment complex.

It takes some looking around, but we're able to find the building and traverse our way up the rickety staircase. Carter knocks on the door a few too many times than I would.

"Hello?" a voice speaks from the inside.

"Police, we need to ask you questions!" Carter speaks up.

Multiple locks are moved around inside the door and it peeks open.

"What do you guys want?" a woman asks.

"We're investigating some deaths, one of them being your son."

"Took you guys long enough," she opens the door, "I was only contacted once about my baby dying!"

"It's been a busy couple of weeks for us."

"Well, kick it into gear."

I look at my watch to make sure we're making time. "Do you have any information about the whereabouts, activities, and contacts your son had prior to his death?"

"He'd started coming home from school later and later and eventually I caught him hanging with some questionable boys passing around plastic bags on one of these streets behind us-"

"Which street?" Carter interrupts.

"8th street, right behind us on one of those power bins."

"Could you describe those kids he was with?"

"Yeah, one of them was pale covered in fake gold and it always looked like he had something in his mouth."

"Anyone else?" I pull out a notepad.

"Yeah, this black kid who he told me never to talk about, and another white kid with brown hair and covered in tattoos up to his jawline."

I flip through the notepad to find a loose photo of one of the suspects. "Is this the kid?"

"Yessir. I don't even want to know who's his mama."

"Anyone else?" Carter asks.

"Just some random kids I see from around the neighborhood."

"Thanks, ma'am, you've been a big help. I'll have someone sent out to ask around the complex."

She slams the door and we continue on our way. "Where you from Carter?"

"It should've said on my file."

"Mississippi or something, right?"

"I'm from Topeka, Kansas."

"Interesting spot—"

"Everything should be written in my file that you need to know about me."

"Don't be so stiff, Carter. If we're working together, then we need to be on good and friendly terms."

"And why is that?"

"I've been in some bad situations more than once, and I've been with a dirty cop or two and that makes it hard to trust your partner in that time of need."

"Boohoo..."

"You'll come around."

A gunshot goes off somewhere, and we both jump into action. We run down the street, I pull out my own gun, and around the corner we find a burglar running at us with a purse and a gun. Carter's reflexes are faster than mine; he points his gun and shouts at him to stop.

"Oh sh—," the robber shouts, turning around to find the woman he probably just stole the purse from. The woman though keeps running and the robber swings behind her to put her in a headlock.

"Imma shoot her, I'll do it," he threatens.

As protocol, we enter the standstill and now have to try to diffuse the situation. The woman grabs his hands trying to pry him off; not a moment later the robber starts convulsing and falls to the ground.

"What'd you just do?" I ask, putting my gun away and Carter keeping it pointed.

The woman, now that I have a good look at her, seems on the younger side, white skin and brown hair; seems pretty average, but I'm sure there's something more.

"Don't arrest me, I'm registered," she informs me backing away with her purse.

"Let me see it," I tell her, "We'll have to file a report though, so I won't let you out of here quite yet."

She digs through her purse to pull out a few cards. She's a PN2, born in '03. "Alright, you check out, but you'll need to stick around for a report."

The whole time the girl was reserved and timid and clearly not wanting to be in public. But the ambulance arrived to pick up the guy and we sent her off after Carter filled out the paperwork. Just another day's work; new leads and another criminal brought to justice.

◌

"How's the case coming?" Sergeant asks me while I type up paperwork on the new information.

"Going slow as always, all our past leads are dead or out of the city and out of our jurisdiction."

"Carter mentioned you got a few new leads though."

"Uh, yeah," I rummage through the folder to pull out a photo of the tattooed suspect that woman pointed out the other day. "Yeah, this kid; he's filed under unnamed in our database."

"Anyways of finding him?" Sergeant asks.

I think of what we have access to, the department lost its permit to use state resources and all their damned cameras. "I have a known repeated location for him, but I don't think he'll be around that place again."

Sergeant holds out his hand, "Let me see that picture, I'll contact some of my friends in the neighboring areas and I'll put out word for this guy."

"He was seen multiple times with Jacob Keens and Gold Mouth in this one complex. If they'd fled, then they should be close by. Some other drug dealers should've taken control of Goldy's trade and shouldn't be too far, but just out of our reach."

Sergeant looks at the photo and puts it on his clipboard. "Seems straightforward. How's it going between you and your new partner?"

"Carter has a cold shoulder, but I feel like I can trust him."

"Good," he says, "I'll let you get back to your paperwork."

I chuckle a little, "Not so much paper anymore."

⊷⊙⊶

Today's my day off; I've been working day and night to try and figure out a way to track that kid with the tattoos down. I always hate going to the state, they make things longer and harder than they need to be. But today's a day off from all that, and I'm going out for some lunch.

So many faces walking up and down these streets sometimes. Some of the kids you wouldn't even know but could knock down entire buildings or make you live a life in a blink of an eye.

I take a breath in from the cigarette and some guy bumps me in the shoulder knocking the tobacco from my mouth. As I look to see who the jerkwad was, it looks like that unnamed suspect with the tattoos, but must just be my tired eyes playing tricks.

I make my way to the coffee shop I like to go to and take a seat at the counter.

"What can I get you detective?" the young man behind the counter asks.

"Blackest coffee you can make and a muffin," I tell him.

"Alright, that'll be $13.96." I give him a large bill and he starts making change.

I lean over to talk quietly to the cashier. "Have you seen any suspicious individuals here lately?"

"No detective, I haven't more than usual," he whispers back.

"Mind if I check your security cameras after my lunch for the front of your store?"

"I'll ask my manager, but the state came in and changed the cameras."

Damn, I think to myself. "Thanks," I respond as I take my bills and coins.

"Your food will be at the next window."

I lazily shove the change in my pocket and walk over to grab my food. "Any creamer sir?" a young lady asks me preparing my drink.

"No thanks, I like it black."

She puts a lid on the cup and puts the muffin on a little paper plate. "Thank you," I reply, taking it along. I walk around the business to try and find a seat. In a place like this at this time of day, you might have to share a table with a stranger, something I've never liked.

Despite my opinion, I sit down in an empty seat across a group of rambunctious teenagers. They all stop what they're doing when they see a cop sit next to them.

"You're not here to arrest us, are you?" one of them asks me.

I take a sip from my hot coffee, "Have you done anything illegal?"

Almost in unison, they shake their heads no. "Then I'm just going to eat my lunch."

I continue on and open up that paper around the muffin and start picking off the nice pieces that are moist and crunchy on the outside, the way I like. The case keeps eating at my mind; most of my leads have been dead ends.

I get close to finishing my meal and the cashier comes over. "My manager said you can come to the back and do what you need to do."

"Thanks," I tell him before downing the rest of the coffee. He leads to the back into his manager's office.

"How's it going detective?" an older man welcomes me, "You said you need our cameras? Unfortunately, the state's been coming in and changing everything so they have control."

"Well, I know your hands're tied, thanks anyways."

"However, the state forgot to cover a blind spot, and I have a personal camera covering the front road that the other store's covering. I can let you take a look at that one."

He opens up a laptop and starts clicking away. "When do you need?"

He let me come by every couple of days, looking through each and every stranger in each frame, looking for anyone I could connect with the main case. I saw a few repeats I had arrested for other crimes, but I was able to catch the tattooed individual come around here about every week or two in the footage. It took a month's worth of days off, but we ran through six months of security video.

Carter and I frequently drove through that street looking for him in a not-so-undercover car. But the progress on busting this drug trade stalled for months with nothing but petty criminals running the drugs with no information to give.

After running through the footage, I had nothing else to follow. On my next day off, I spent some time at the death site of Jacob Keens.

Some of the bricks are still lying around and the hole in the wall was never patched up. Nothing new here, everything's been looked over and cleaned. No more new evidence here; case closed.

◂◂ ⊙ ▸▸

For the first time in a while, Carter comes into my office tossing something on my desk. "What's this about? I never heard about this during school."

It's an announcement flyer for the department to attend the annual briefing on the most current scientific research and advancements. "It's for those science jackasses to tell us about the research they're doing. It's not supposed to happen for another four months."

I take the flyer and head to Sergeant's office. "What's this about; it hasn't been a year yet."

"They appealed to the state to make it semi-annual since they're 'making extraordinary advancements' or the sorts," he tells me.

"I hate looking at those people, and now I have to do it two times a year?"

Sergeant chuckles, "I hate them too, but clearly not as much as you."

I sigh and walk back to my office to be stopped by some of the officers moving a cuffed teenager with a special blindfold and mouth cover into the questioning room.

"What's this about?" I ask one of them, "Aren't those supposed to be used to transport to high security?"

"This kid was found in a closet after he killed all of his classmates when the cops arrived."

"Mind if I watch?"

"If there's space in the back."

I watch as they move him into the interrogation room and have him face away from the one-way window. They instruct him to remove his mouth cover when they leave, and he does as he's told.

"Can you explain to us what happened?" one of the cops asks over the intercom.

The poor kid just starts crying and shakes his head no. "You can't hurt anyone in there. You have to tell us what happened before we can do anything else."

"I-I," the kid starts sobbing, "I was just reading in front of the class and when I looked up—"

"What happened when you looked up?"

"I-I looked up, an-and there was blood everywhere and all my friends—"

They look at me, "You know what classification this falls under?"

"Closest thing I can think of is PN, but some of these new ones are getting harder to classify. I think this kid might be a new one, I'll find out during this next conference."

"What level do you think?" she asks.

I think about it how closely this matches up with PN. "The highest the official classification goes is 5, but killing an entire school class without even touching them doesn't match up with level 5."

"We'll have to call the state science department," one of them says to another.

I really hate calling them; these kids just become guinea pigs and are locked away for the rest of their lives. I can't think of anything else I can do for the poor kid. "I can fill out the paperwork for you guys, it's better than what I have to do."

"Sure, why not?"

"Be sure to keep this kid safe," I tell them, "There's a lot of criminals who'd like to get their hands on him."

"We'll have to move him to solitary for that."

They hand me a bunch of documents for the kid and I take them back to my office. Poor kid; the rest of his life just got ruined.

The now semi-annual conference is just an excuse for the state to waste our time updating us on every little thing those science jerkwads do. I'm glad I only have to be there for eight hours instead of the whole week.

I walk through the doors with Carter a little bit behind me and snatch the pamphlets by the door, glancing over them as I find a seat. And then I see the head jackass: Dr. Barthold Cannonburry, head of scientific research for the state and consultant for the federal government.

"Wonderful to see you all here," he starts to announce, "Let's not waste time."

They start to present some important findings. Turns out many people with 25 have extra organs or something that becomes the source of their abilities. Removing this organ also doesn't always remove this ability and the organ almost never grows in a consistent spot in the body or in a consistent size. On top of the inconsistency, not all of them even have one.

Knowing this, they developed some new kind of bullet that hones onto people with this organ, giving us an advantage if we ever have to try and fight.

Along with some useless information, they detail a map and timeline. The births of the Tenty-fivers eerily resembles that of the spread of disease starting slow in Greenland back in 2099 and skyrocketing once births starting appearing in more populated areas.

"You'll be getting a new list of classifications," he says, "Some of the changes include an expanded leveling system and more detailed requirements for each level and each classification. That concludes the semi-annual conference."

"You said this happens twice a year now?" Carter leans over to ask.

"Yup," I reply.

Carter dawns a face of disgust, "Damn."

The lights turn back on and everyone begins to leave. As I walk to the exit, I see Dr. Cannonburry ushering the door in the back. "Ah, Detective Jameson!" he calls out to me.

I raise my middle finger and try to walk past him, "You've already wasted eight hours of my time; not a second more."

"I don't see it as a waste. After all, I'm actually trying to solve this problem."

I step up into his face, "By unethical experiments and creating new ways to torture and kill these poor kids?"

"Everything is approved by the federal government and whatever's left of the United Nations."

"Move and stop wasting our time."

He slides to his right, giving us a path to the exit. "I hope you're partner is doing well."

I lift my hand above my shoulder and flip him off as Carter and I and the rest of the people here leave.

◄ɪ ⊙ ɪ►

Carter and I drive past Jacob Keens' death site just to find some latent press and past that coffee shop to try and find the tattooed individual.

To break the silence, I ask Carter a question. "You have a family Carter?"

"Yes."

"How many?"

"My wife and I."

"No kids?"

"No," he tells me, bringing our conversation to a halt.

We continue to drive through the busy street in silence and traffic slows to a standstill. Carter starts looking intensely at the crowd. "That's him!" he shouts, bolting out of the car.

I twist the key and run out too, following Carter. It takes a moment but I lock my gaze on the man running the crowd causing a commotion. "Police!" Carter shouts pulling out his gun.

Not two minutes in and I'm already out of breath, but Carter keeps running after him. We keep running until we hit a street with warehouses on each corner, and the suspect runs right into an abandoned one.

"I'll go in from the side, you go after him," Carter says as he taps my shoulder and banks to the side of the building

I try and keep up the running into where the kid ran into. This building is abandoned with lots of places to hide; dust floating everywhere.

"Police!" I shout out, "Come out with your hands above your head!"

I pull out my gun with these new-fangled bullets when I start hearing footsteps echo around me. The kid comes speeding from behind a crate, running faster than my own reflexes. A bullet fires and I get knocked to the ground by the tremendous force of this kid running into me.

"Come on old man," he taunts me, "I got speed for days."

I pick my gun back up and get back to my feet, and Carter sneaks up behind him. "Stop right there, kid."

He starts charging at me, and Carter fires a bullet through his leg. The kid tackles me to the ground and limps across the open space. "You're partner here too?"

"Police!" Carter shouts walking from behind an entirely different crate.

The kid starts running again, but this time, he's running away. Carter fires a bullet and it curves through the air like nothing I've ever seen and hits the kid in lower right of his back. Carter, like a real cop, runs over and starts to arrest him.

"Damn kid," I say aloud, "You should've played football."

◄┼ ⊙ ┼►

"So, what are you going to tell us?" I ask him.

"Not a damned thing," he snarks.

I take a sip of water and watch as Carter finally makes it here after all the paperwork. "Not a damn thing, huh?"

"Nope."

"You understand the crimes we can connect you with and how much jail time you'll get?"

"I have an idea."

Carter silently makes his way behind the kid and grasps his shoulder. "Are you sure?" Carter asks.

The kid gets startled and nearly falls out of his chair. "Hell yes."

"There are people dying because of the crime organization you work for. You know that? All these innocent kids, dead."

"Nobody's innocent detective," he replies, "Y'know what? I will tell you something; All this your chasing? It's a tip of an iceberg of deep-seeded corruption, crime, and drugs."

I take another sip of my water. "If you don't comply here—"

"Go ahead and tell me what's going to happen."

"We'll have to move you to high security for interrogation."

The kid laughs, "You think I'm scared of that place?"

I knock my water over onto his hands and it flows down into his lap. "You're making a mistake kid. I could've helped," I say as I walk out.

We had high security come in and transfer him for interrogation by the state. I didn't hear anything after that for another two weeks, signature of state protocol and laziness. But just like that, my very last lead is gone. This case has finally regressed to ground zero. After those two weeks, I finally got a long-awaited letter from the state saying they got absolutely nothing from him, sealed like an old pickle jar.

Sergeant comes into my office with not a word escaping his lips. As soon as he closes the door, he starts speaking. "Your last suspect was found dead in high security, head twisted nearly 180."

I shove the papers in my hands to the side. "This ain't no prank, is it?"

"No, sir."

I refrain from being too vulgar in front of Sergeant, but might as well close this case or move it to state.

"But," he continues, "I put in a request for the use of state cameras and it just got approved."

"Thank Jemima," I whisper, "When am I scheduled?"

"Tomorrow at five in the morning."

"Couldn't think it'd be all good news."

⏸ ⊙ ⏸

The worker leads me into a dark room with twenty some odd monitors all turned off. "You have access to thirty minutes of footage from one camera. Do you know when and where?"

"Yeah, February 17th, 9:00 AM, corner of Ophelia and Compass on the front of the building," I tell him. Jacob's death isn't sitting well with me, there has to be something more.

The worker starts working on the computer looking through maps and databases or something beyond my level of skill. "This building?"

I shake my head. "Which angle do you want?"

There's a camera that points directly at the entrance of the building. I point and say, "That one."

"That one's off-limits."

"Whaddya mean it's off-limits?"

"It's off-limits," he repeats.

There's another that barely has the front in view and I point at it. "Alright," he says clicking away and moving through computer programs.

The video plays, and it's nothing that surprises me; people walking around and then an explosion going off and scattering the people. Nothing new, nothing I can use. I've wasted this opportunity. The video plays out and then sirens signal the police arriving.

The video plays through and I've learned nothing. The video repeats and for a brief moment, I see navy blue legs at the very edge of the screen. "Can you rewind the footage a couple of seconds?"

"This is all the footage you've been given access to."

I snap. Everything I've done for this case, for years now leading to this dickhead stopping me right in my tracks. I grab his shirt and start shoving him to a wall. "I have been working on this case for two damn years! People have died, and I'm getting to the bottom. Now rewind the damn video four goddamn seconds!"

"four seconds, and that's it," he says, and I let go. He scans a card and presses a button a few times. Frame by frame and this mystery man is revealed; the blue legs turn into blue pants turn into a police uniform. And the back of the head of that man is unmistakable.

"That's all I need," I tell the man, grabbing my coat and heading for the exit.

⊩⊙⊪

"I need to go investigate something, mind if I head out?" I ask Sargent.

"Is Carter free to go with you?" he replies.

"I actually need to be solo on this one."

Sargent pause and thinks for a little. "Just be safe out there."

"Will do," I assure him, "Oh, and congrats on the baby. I didn't know your wife was pregnant."

He laughs, "Thanks, she wanted to keep it under wraps."

I take my personal car over to the building where Jacob Keens met his demise. No badge, no uniform, just a concealed gun. Traffic seems worse than usual right now, but I get there. I find somewhere to park and walk up to the front door with my coat's collar flipped high. A few knocks on the door, and the owner opens up.

"An' you are?" he asks.

"I'm a detective, can I come in?"

"Why?"

"I need to recheck the crime scene."

"Ya'mean that giant-ass hole on the side insurance won' cover?"

"Yessir."

The man sighs and waves me in. He points me down a hallway to the door leading to the crime scene. But something new catches my eyes. A brass doorknob deformed and burned black.

"Did you flip the door handle after the crime?" I ask.

"Ya, some reason t'was lockin' from out here."

"You mean it wasn't supposed to do that in the first place?"

"Nah, 'tis a livin' space."

"Who rented the room?"

"Some dumbass wit' gold teeth."

I pull out my notebook and start writing down some important information. "Did you have a cop stop by the day of the incident?"

"You serious?" he starts telling me, "Cops swarming this whole street!"

"What about right before?" I show him a photo of the possible dirty cop.

"Ya, he came in a few hours before. He said he needed to check the room an' I wasn' allowed to look. Ya'know, he prolly the one who switched the door thingamajig."

"Thanks, that's all I need; you've given me valuable information."

I walk out and make my way to my car, writing down everything I could possibly think of relating to this case and linking the dirty cop to most of the dead ends.

Once I'm done, I pull out my personal phone and start dialing in a number to someone I'd never thought I'd have to call: a whistleblower.

"Well, hello Jameson," he greets me.

"Meet me at my coffee shop," I order, promptly hanging up.

The drive is awkward and silent with the feeling someone's watching me. Knowing the state, someone is, but I at least don't see anyone following me in person.

"I'd never would've thunk I'd ever get a call from you detective," he starts ranting at the corner of the shop, "I thought I was on that list of 'Never Call.'"

"You are," I say, tossing my notebook to him, "Put all this out at the start of next week if you don't hear from me."

I promptly keep walking into the shop like nothing happened and order some coffee. As I make my first step past the door, my vision goes dark.

◀◀ ⊙ ▶▶

I slowly wake up to feel like my face hit the pavement and something pounds my stomach. I try to satiate the tickle on my upper lip to find I'm cuffed down to something on the ground, but I have enough mobility to press down on some gauze and feel the immense pain underneath.

"You're finally up," I hear Carter say.

"He's up now mister, can I leave now," some little kid whimpers.

"No," Carter replies. I open my eyes to see Carter in normal clothes pointing a gun at me.

"Did you seriously shoot me?" I ask.

"You started attacking me outside the coffee shop."

Carter must've dragged me to one of the abandoned warehouses, but I don't know why I blacked out. "You're making a mistake Carter—"

"Oh am I?" he cuts me off.

"I need to go," the kid whines again.

"Let the kid go, Carter."

Carter turns around and starts waving the gun to make the kid leave, but as the kid starts running away the gun fires. I'm forced to watch as the body hits the ground.

"So you're a part of this too?" I ask.

"No, but I know who is."

"Sergeant?" I try and confirm my suspicion.

"Do you know what it's like to be one of us? '25s' as we're called?" Carter asks.

"Is Sergeant dirty!?" I demand, but the bullet wound in my stomach starts giving sharp pains.

"That new organ they were discussing at the conference, my son had one. Or at least would've if it hadn't assimilated into his brain stem and killed him."

"Carter, I'm sorry, but I need to know how far—"

Carter cuts me off, "My wife couldn't take it a moment longer, and shot herself a couple of weeks ago."

"Carter!" I keep demanding past the pain.

"I was abused both inside and outside the house because of something I had no control over. Not even abilities to speak of. But none of that's something that would be written in a file, would it?"

"Tell me how deep this goes, Carter!"

"Sergeant's baby has 25, I bet you didn't know that."

I feel something pop inside me, probably a blood clot. "The more of a threat we seem to the world, the faster they'll find a cure. That's why you've been put on this wild goose chase, to make us seem like the bad guy, and I just a shining example.

"And now, you're just another dead dirty cop to the public, with me having to put you down with a kid in the crossfire."

Warm blood starts to pool beneath me and I start slipping away. "You're making a big mistake Carter," I try to persuade him.

"What's the worst that can happen, Detective? My family and I get separated?"

My breathing slows down and I start blacking out again.

"It seems that you've caught me monologuing, sorry you couldn't finish your coffee, Detective," Carter says as he promptly fires a bullet through his own leg. They all made a mistake; it didn't have to go this way.

The Fate of Two Brothers

⇜ ◎ ⇝

WITH ONE hand, I thrust my sword into his abdomen; with the other, I draw him close as he pushes his enchanted sword likewise through me. "We were born together, we'll die together," he mutters into my ear, his tears flowing down onto my face.

"Tell me, brother," I let my inner demon response, "Do you fear Death?"

I twist my sword around as I shove him away. He falls into the stream running opposite the cavern. Meanwhile, I've lost too much blood, my legs crumble and I fall between two rock formations.

"Dying is a natural part of life, and if it means stopping you from losing your soul forever, I'll happily accept it."

My demons begin to speak for me again, "I do not fear dying, for my being will exist forever. But all should fear Death."

We both began to cough blood; I let it flow down. "It's not too late for you, come back," he tells me.

I cup my hands and begin to fill them with the blood flowing from my wounds. "Never again will I lower myself," I reply as I paint the incantations over my face.

"Please don't do this," he begs.

The demon whispers in my ears the spells I need to cast on my dying body and willingly repeat the words. As I speak them, the blood begins to burn the spells on my skin.

The world around me begins to fade to black as Death envelops me, but the last thing I hear is my foolish brother crawling through the bloodstained water, trying in his last gasps of life to steal my salvation.

◄‖ ⊙ ‖►

My stone flies through the air and hits the base of the stick we stuck into the ground for our game. Brother hurls his stone and it bounces off mine and lands outside the circle we drew.

"Ha ha, I win!" I shout.

"No fair, mine bounced away," brother complains, trying to push me down. As I stumble backward, I trip over a tree root and fall to the ground.

"Mom!" I cry out, holding my elbow. I look behind me as I hear mother approaching us, but it's not mother who I see.

"Are you okay," the mystery girl asks me, "You seem to have fallen."

"Who are you?" I ask; she must've not been a few years older than us.

Another mystery man walks up, carrying a staff with a disintegrating metal plate mounted on the side. "I brought you these two, I forgot who's who."

The woman brushed her long black hair out of her face revealing pale skin. "I'm just wandering through, and I heard you two playing."

"He's just being a sore loser," I tell her, throwing a wad of grass at brother.

"Perhaps I should teach him to be a little more humble," she says as she walks to brother and takes his hand, "Why don't we go play, and I won't be as mean to you."

Brother happily goes along and blows raspberries at me.

"No!" my demons and I scream out.

I heard the crack of steel against stone and the grassland shifts into white sand and a silver sky with a single moon glaring down. The man's hand clasps my shoulder and pulls me back.

"No! Take me!" I cry out.

"Nonrec's made her decision. I'm just here to drag you to the afterlife."

I try to run and trade fates with my brother, but this man slams his staff into the ground. The staff sprouts four limbs and chains secure themselves around my appendages and my throat. One of my demons begins to crawl and whispers curses into my ear.

"No!" I cry out, "That's supposed to be me!"

I start to run, but these chains hold back as if I were nothing but air.

"Stop struggling," The man says, "I have to drag you to the afterlife, and it doesn't look like it's going to be a good one for you."

He pulls his staff and drags me away against my will, my feet dragging into the sand and the demons begin to devour my soul for the eternity that lies ahead. I scream out once again.

I hear in the distance that mystery girl saying to my brother's soul, "I think I'll call you Necron, and we'll be friends for a *very* long time."

Grandpa's Old Shed

⫷◎⫸

AFTER SIX long hours of driving, I've finally arrived at my grandfather's estate. He died about a month ago, but the family is only now beginning to deal with his hoarding problem. Grandpa decided to buy a five-bedroom house when he first got married, but his wife left only a few short years later and he just filled his life with boxes and rooms full of junk.

After so many decades of all of us telling him to get rid of all of it, it's finally happening. All of it has to be gone in less than a month for the sale of the house, and I'm the one who has to make all that happen. Maybe I could get the local Mormons or scouts to help?

He had plenty of photos and clothes he would buy for all the kids in the family, but he would always forget about them; one of the rooms is even full of books. So many books, but he hated reading. Though he did love hunting, he bought a new gun fairly often. Even though he had a house this big, he still built a dumb little shed for even more of his stuff.

It takes all afternoon to do it, but most of all this junk is cataloged for sale or donation. The sun's finally setting, which means the shed should be cooling down.

That shed has been renovated more times than any shed should, ever since ten or fifteen years ago. I think he stored his meat and hunted game inside, but nobody was allowed in there to see.

The shed door still creaks, but the lights still work; he must've paid the electrical bill a few months out; sounds like something he'd do. A squirrel or something scatters about, but I pay no attention to it and keep cataloging everything. This is where he kept all his guns and bullets for hunting. I'm surprised the smell in here isn't worse from what he said he kept here.

"I should probably take these guns inside," I tell myself, "Not-so-safe to keep them behind an unlocked door."

I put the clipboard underneath my arm and start grabbing all the rifles and a few shotguns.

"Abe?" I hear a girl say. I drop the guns and turn around startled, patting myself down for a knife or something.

"Abe?" she asks again, "is that you?"

I look around to try and find the voice, but I don't really see anyone hiding behind anything. I pick up one of the guns, hoping it's loaded when the light's cut out.

I prop open the door to let a little light into the shed, and the beam of light casts about the wall. "You're not Abe."

"I have no clue who Abe is," I say, "You need to come out now!"

I walk back to prop open the door a little more. "Who are you?" the shaky voice asks.

There's a silhouette of a girl towards the back of the shed. "You need to get out of here, it's not okay to prank a dead man's family."

The light creeps closer to her, and instantly she cowers in the corner behind a pile of stuff.

I drop the gun and say, "Alright kid, time to get out of here."

I kick open the door fully and the light shines directly on her revealing a curled teenager with long black hair. She starts screaming bloody murder and trying to hide from the light. "Kid—"

"Close it!" she cries, "Please!"

I set down the gun on the counter and flip another light on. She keeps begging for the door to be closed, so I just let it swing itself shut. I walk over to see her pale skin covered in burns and scratches trembling behind a broken refrigerator. She knocks the fridge door open and suddenly I'm overpowered by the smell rotten meat.

She starts sobbing and curls up into the dusty corner. "Is Abe dead?" She asks me through her tears.

"I don't know who Abe is."

"The old guy who lives here," she tells me, "I haven't seen him in weeks."

"The guy who lived here was my grandfather, Martin," I explain, "He died a month ago."

She starts trembling and sobbing even harder. "Look, kid, you have to go somewhere, you can't stay here."

"He used to take care of me," she says through her tears, "I don't know where to go."

This is a bad situation; I have to drive home in a few days and now there's a homeless girl living in my grandpa's old shed. "Look, I can take you to the hospital or something, but you can't stay here."

"No, no, no, no," she utters to herself, "I can't go anywhere, they'll find me."

"The hell is going on? Are you high?"

She goes on and on about 'them'. "You need to keep me safe, like *he* did."

"I don't know how you knew my grandpa, but I can't just adopt you out of his shed."

"Please," she begs, grabbing ahold of my shirt.

I let out a sigh, and slowly push her away. "I can let you sleep in a bed tonight, but I can't just take you in."

She latches back onto my legs, crying. "Please don't let them find me."

A stream of light from the setting sun creeps onto her hand, forming a rash and hives on her skin.

"Come on, I'll let you inside," I tell her.

She backs away in her tears, cradling her hand behind a broken fridge and says, "I can't be in the light."

I look at my watch; the sun should be set in a few minutes. I look back at her to see her in a trance of some sort, whispering to herself, "blood."

"Hey," I exclaim, "Let's get you inside."

I grab her by the hand, and she slips back into reality, but she's trembling like a dog and stumbling side to side. I lead her out when we walk past an overgrown bush, just when something begins to rustle about inside; her eyes lose all humanity and dilate like some sort of predator and she jumps into the bush after the noise.

I chase after her, but she's fast. She stops short of another overgrown shrub, and I hear the sounds of snapping bones. I rush over to grab her, but I'm greeted by the sight of her biting down into the corpse of a squirrel with the blood draining down her chin.

She begins to drink the blood flowing from the wounded animal, and I'm thoroughly concerned. "Hey!" I shout. She's acting like an addict, but this is a new level of dependence.

Her head lifts up with the look of a hungry wild animal. Blood drips down from her mouth as she looks around for something else to maim. Silently, I watch as she snatches a bird from the air and bites into until it stops moving.

The blood drains slowly and she begins to drifts back into sanity. Her eyes become more and more human and her body begins bobbing back and forth like a crying child. Tears well up in her eyes, and she drops the dead bird on the ground.

"The hell?" I whisper, "What in the actual hell are you?"

She begins whimpering and says, "Your grandpa kept me safe. Please keep me safe too."

◄◄ ⊙ ►►

I sniff the nearly expired coffee and take a big swig, putting to rest the fact that it was indeed expired. "You're a vampire?" I ask.

She lowers her head and continues wiping the blood from her face. She looks so ashamed for some reason.

"And, as a vampire, you need to drink blood," I begin to try and piece together the story, "Is that why you ate the squirrel?"

She nods. "Are you like this every time you see an animal? Or people?"

"No," she tells me, "Blood is like a drug where the addiction only gets worse and never goes away. I need it."

"Do you need it, like, every day or on occasion?"

"Abe helped me get it down to every two weeks, but I haven't had any since he died."

I sit down and force down more of the coffee. "Naturally, I have more questions, but I'll save them for another day.

"But I do need to know who 'them' is and why my grandpa kept you safe from these people."

"Other vampires," She says, "They're pure animals; savages. I think I was turned when I was a teenager, but Abe captured me and brought me back to humanity from that."

"You think?" I ask, "Do you not remember before?"

"Once upon a time, I was a savage, an animal. It really messes with your head. I don't remember much from before."

I take a deep breath and try to understand all this. "Do vampires need to sleep?"

"Yeah, but I usually sleep during the day; I'm still a little shaken."

I look over to see that rash on her hand from earlier has subsided and she's trembling from head to toe. "Well, grandpa has rooms full of books and clothes," I tell her, "So clean up and help yourself."

"Thanks," She says, wiping more blood and curling up.

"Food's in the fridge too if vampires eat food."

I head into the living room to lie down on the plastic covered sofa. Her shadows move about as she passes in front of the lights. There's an old portrait of Grandpa and Grandma above the fireplace. So many secrets, what kind of life did he live? New guns, clothes, and books he couldn't use, and a shed that no one could look inside.

I really shouldn't've had that coffee, it most definitely was bad and now I'm not going to get any sleep. If only the alcohol wasn't gone or expired.

A steam hammer hits a pipe and shakes some dust off the ceiling into my face. The water starts running and footsteps make their way around the upstairs.

I try to close my eyes to sleep, but she comes back down after a five-minute shower. The girl comes walking down the stairs dressed in some of the clothes stored in the room.

She slowly makes her way to another chair on the other side of the room with a book in her hand.

"The clothes fit you well."

"Abe bought me a lot of clothes," she replies, "He bought so many things to not make people think there was somebody he was taking care of. He bought the books to keep me entertained."

"Makes better sense than him forgetting to give away all that stuff for fifteen years."

"I didn't know he had a family."

"Well, clearly he kept a lot of secrets."

She curls up in a chair and opens the book, but she just sits there staring at the pages as she trembles.

"Still shaken up?" I ask.

She nods and sets the book aside. "I haven't had blood in a long time, so I'm kind of messed up from that. I'm guessing you had too much of that coffee?"

"Yup," I say, "But it was expired, and so was the beer."

Some of her hair falls in front of her face, and a tear strolls down her cheek.

"Don't feel too bad, kid. He was old as rocks and too old to be hunting every week."

"What?" she asks.

"It was a hunting accident," I explain, "He loved to hunt."

She covers her mouth and starts sobbing. "Hey, what's wrong?"

She stands and starts running for the door. I run after her, but my stomach turns sideways. I chase her through the front room, and she just barrels through the door into the night.

"Hey!" I call out to her. She's so fast, but she trips on a fallen branch and hits the ground. I catch up and try to grab ahold of her.

She thrashes around and starts dragging me behind on the ground through a bush.

"Hey!" I shout, "Stop!"

She trips again and falls into a dead shrub. I get on my feet and try to pull her out, tearing some of her clothes. But she just curls up and starts crying.

She says something through her tears, and it takes me a moment to figure out what she said. "He died because of me."

⊷⊙⊶

I pick her up in my arms and try to carry her back into the house. She clings to me, crying her eyes out, but somehow keeps rambling on through the tears.

We make our way into the house and I set her down on the couch. "What was that?" I ask.

Through her tears, she says, "He always hunted to bring me blood and food. He died because of me."

I sit down next to her and try to comfort her. Grandpa really did live a strange life. And now I'm thrown headfirst into all the mess he left behind. This is some serious government type secret stuff.

"Look, kid," I say, "It's not your fault—"

She glares up at me, "I'm not a kid; I was born May 1964."

I resume my words of solace, "It wasn't your fault, he was way too old to be doing what he did without help."

She starts crying once again. "I don't know what to do without him."

"I'll help you figure something out," I promise her, "In the meanwhile I need to continue prepping the house for sale."

I stand up and start walking up the stairs to start packing away all his junk. It all just comes out to be boxes and boxes of books, and somehow, not a single one is the same size as another.

This room is full of books, filled to the ceiling; no shelves or tables, just packed to the brim with dusty books. Hours go by in silence of me building the boxes and slowly packing the books one by one.

The sun starts peeking through the window and shining through the stacks. Just then, something crashes downstairs followed by the girl screaming her lungs out. I rush down, nearly tripping down the stairs myself to find her squirming around underneath the table like she's being burned alive as the sunlight casts through the windows.

I rush to close the blinds, but one of them gets stuck. I grab a tablecloth sitting on the counter, and toss it underneath the table. The table is over a hundred years old and heavier than I can lift.

She screams in pain, writhing around underneath the table I'm too weak to move. "It burns!" she cries.

"Well, I don't know what to do!" I yell back to her.

She rushes to cover herself with the cloth and tries to cover herself as she writhes around.

"What do I do?!"

I hear one of the wooden legs crack as the table slides across the room. She shouts back, "I don't know!"

She's moving around uncontrollably, but I manage to lift her up in my arms and I run across the house to the room adjoined to the living room, where there's one window covered by firewood outside.

I try to set her down gently, but she jerks around and I end up dropping her in the dark corner of the room. I watch in horror as she writhes around on the ground in agony, but there's nothing I can do, and I back away into the other room slowly closing the door behind me. It's just too hard to watch, too painful.

I toss her a couple of tubes of burn cream from across the room as I walk to her.

"This is all I could find," I tell her.

"I lost track of time tonight," she replies, "I didn't realize the sun was out."

"Quick question," I say sitting down beside her, "Can you heal fast like in comic books?"

She gives me a look mixed between offense and stupidity on my part and starts applying the cream all around her body. "That's a stupid question. It'll take me few weeks for all the burns to be gone."

"That's still pretty fast."

"It's all I've ever known."

I lay my head back against the wall, trying to think of a way I'm supposed to deal with all of this. "Do you eat normal food?"

"Why wouldn't I?" she retorts.

"Look, I'm not exactly equipped to handle all this here. So I'm going to take you to my home and talk this over with the missus. If you don't mind that is."

"This is my home."

"Then please tell me what it is I'm supposed to do," I say, "Because I have no frickin' clue."

She sits in silence with only the sound of burn cream in my head.

"I'm going to make a couple phone calls if the lines are still working and eat some food if there's some that hasn't gone bad."

She sits there in silence and sadness, staring at the sun streak cast about the wall. "Hold down the fort while I'm busy."

I walk back into the living room where there's a phone mounted on the center post and start dialing for my oldest sister. It makes the dated buzzing sound and a pop before she answers

"Who is this?" she asks, "It's not polite to use a dead—"

"It's me, Jess," I interrupt.

"What do you want?"

"I've run into a situation—"

"Then deal with it, we're all tired of cleaning up your mess."

"It's urgent, and I need you to finish up packing all of grandpa's stuff."

"No. You got the luck of the draw on this one, and it's your responsibility."

"Jess, this is really serious. I have to deal with this, and I won't be able to prep the house in time."

"Not my problem."

"Hey!" I yell into the phone as she hangs up, "Shoot."

I start dialing for my youngest brother. None of us talk all the much in the past recent years, but Kyle's always been responsive.

"Hello?" I hear from the other side.

"Kyle, it's me," I say.

"Hey," he says, "What do you need?"

"A situation's come up," I try to vaguely explain, "It's pretty urgent, and I can't finish preparing the house."

"It's your responsibility."

"Kyle," I beg, "This is serious. I need you to finish."

He sighs over the phone. "Did you at least pack all the books?"

"Most of them, and I've got mostly everything cataloged for sale."

He sighs one more time, "What happened? Why can't you finish this?"

I look over to the room where the girl is. "You'll just have to trust me."

"You of all people should know why that's hard to do," he reminds me.

"Just trust me, this is serious."

The speaker pops again and I hear some chatter on the other side. "I need a full explanation after it's taken care of," he tells me, "But Jen and I will head over there in the morning to finish up."

"Thanks so much, Kyle. You're a lifesaver."

"Well, I was a paramedic," he replies before the phone cuts out and I slide the reciever back onto the wall.

I walk back to the front door, where there's a bowl full of junk. There are some magazines, snacks, and some more. But underneath, there's a huge baton flashlight.

It's big and hefty, and the light's crazy bright when I turn it on. I toss it around to see how hard it is to swing, but I just end up blasting my eyes with the light.

"Please turn that off," the girl says as she wraps herself in a space blanket.

I flip off the switch and ask, "Are you cold?"

"It keeps the sunlight off," she replies, "That's one of Abe's UV lights he keeps around."

"My Grandpa had more than one of these?"

"He would keep me safe from other vampires," she explains, "He used those when he had a few run-ins and fights."

"Are the other vampires the 'them' he kept you safe from?"

She nods and steps away from the moving sunbeam.

"So he was a vampire hunter?" I think aloud, "Alright so here's what's going to happen.

"I'm going to have to take you to my home and have my wife help me with all this. I'm in no way equipped to keep you safe here.

"Now that you've been dumped in my lap, I have no frickin' idea what to do. My wife is usually the one to think of everything."

"So what now?" she asks, "What about tomorrow or the day after?"

I toss the flashlight on the couch, "I have no idea. I've literally been thrown into a world where vampires exist yesterday.

"But all I've got right now is to take you home and figure this out there."

She turns away and walks back into the room. "I'm just going to sleep and hope I can think of something better when I wake up."

"Well, unless you do, we'll have to leave when the sun sets."

⊷ ⦿ ⊶

Bushes rustle around in the distance as I continue cleaning and cataloging before we leave. I see some animals scatter into the forest when I turn. The sun finally starts setting below the mountainless horizon.

She comes out from the door of the old house. "You think of anything while you were asleep?" I ask.

I see here shaking and her eyes are darting around wildly the landscape. "Hey?" I try to catch her attention.

"Hey!" I walk up to her and grab her shoulder. Her pupils dilate and focus on me.

Suddenly, she comes back to life and starts blinking and bobbing her head in exhaustion. "It's not safe here anymore," she says.

"What was that?"

She starts dozing off from exhaustion and is still trembling. "What's what?" she retorts.

I roll my eyes and lead her back inside. "Are you okay?"

"Uh," she still dazed, "I'm just—I was using some of my vampire abilities; I get a little dizzy after I use them, it's hard to do it for me now."

I snap my fingers around her face to see if she can follow the noises, but she acts drunk. "We're heading out now, grab some clothes."

She nods in acknowledgment and stumbles around up the stairs while I make sure the last door is locked. I walk to the front door and grab one the flashlight off the couch. I make my way to the back while she's still getting clothes and I try to shut off the main electric panel, but the switch is jammed on.

A closer look reveals a small piece of wood underneath the switch. I try wiggling it out, but it won't budge either. I pull out my knife and try to break it out, finally the wood snaps and flies past my head along with all the power shutting off in the house.

All the lights go off and the whirring of some machines shut down. The power has been running since he's been gone, until now at least.

I go back inside to see the girl lugging down a packed suitcase. "What's in that one?"

Tears run down her face, and she responds in a shaky voice. "An emergency kit, I just stuffed some extra clothes into it."

I stop to think about all this. All this craziness was grandpa's life, and now I'm in it. "Alight, toss it into the back of the red truck. We should make it home before sunrise, and when we make it back you hunker down in the basement for now."

She nods and stumbles outside, and I'm behind her locking the door. More of the foliage begins to rustle around. I shine the light into the bushes and whatever's in there scatters away.

She throws the luggage into the bed of the truck and we both get in. I look over to see her bobbing her head, but she manages to get the seatbelt on. I twist the ignition and we go off on our way.

A few moments of silence is all I can take, so I try to start talking. "So," I ramble, "Do you have a name?"

"Probably," she replies, "Abe called me Sarah."

"Do you want everyone to call you Sarah?"

"I don't really know."

The car hits a bump. "Well, how about we just stick with it, *Sarah.*"

She eventually falls asleep, and not even the car jerking around from the rough road wakes her. But then I notice another car behind us. We're in the middle of nowhere, on the interstate, but they're getting closer until we're nearly touching bumpers.

I roll down the window and wave my hand for them to pass, but they just stay behind us. After a while of the lights in my eyes, I pull over. To my surprise, they pull over behind us. I wave my hand again, but they stay seated.

"I don't have time to waste," I say to myself, getting out to walk over there, being sure to lock the door and take that flashlight with me.

I walk over and knock on the window. When it rolls down, I'm greeted with a young fellow, alone in the car. "You goin' somewhere?" I ask.

"Just down this interstate," he replies.

"Is there a reason you pulled over?"

"Just saw you pull over, thought I should be here if your car broke down."

"Well, My car's just fine, so why don't you go on right ahead."

"Oh, well, I'm not going any faster than—"

"I insist."

He looks aggravated about me calling him out on following us, but silently, he goes off into the night. The tires spin out, throwing dirt about as he drives away.

I get back into my car, seeing that the girl is still out cold, but I just sit there for a few minutes to get some distance. But eventually, we do make it through the night into town. She woke up at some point but was completely silent when I found her in awe of the city lights.

⇤ ⊙ ⇥

I can see the sun shining behind the mountain, but we're already so close; we entered the city only a few moments ago. I shake the girl until I get her attention. "You got another one of those space blankets?"

"A what?"

"The blanket you were wearing yesterday, do you have another one?" I ask.

"No, that was the last one."

I breathe in and start pushing down on the accelerator, hoping I don't get pulled over. But we make our way to the house just in time before the sun is barely peeking over the hills.

"Alright, the sun's almost here," I tell her, "Let's be quick about getting you downstairs."

I unlock the doors and grab my keys. I rush to the door and unlock it. I shout to her, "Hurry up! It's the door behind the stairs!"

I look back, and she's taking her sweet time admiring the new landscape. "Hey!" I yell, "Sun's here now!"

She recollects and speedily runs through the door into the house. It doesn't look like anyone's home or awake, which means I'll have to explain why she's here first thing after I see everyone.

She looks around, slowly wandering towards the basement door. I go back to grab the baggage when I realize my wife's car is gone.

When I go back inside with the suitcase in hand, I see two of my young daughters standing at the top of the stairs. "Who's that?" Lila asks, pointing to Sarah frozen in surprise in the basement doorway.

"That's a homeless girl we're going to help out for a few days, Lila," I try to explain, "It's a little early to be up, don't you think?"

"Tina's the one who woke me up," she replies.

"Shut up," Tina pushes Lila a little bit.

"And where's Julie? Did you wake her up too?"

They both giggle, "She was mad, so she went back to bed."

I set the luggage by the downstairs door, and notice some sunlight casting itself through the windows. "Go on down, I'll be there in a moment," I tell Sarah.

"I didn't know you had kids," she retorts before heading into the darkness.

"Do either of you two know when your mom's coming back home?" I ask the kids.

Lila scratches her head, "She said she's out shopping for food."

I walk over to them and greet them properly. "This early?"

"Julie said she really wanted pancakes before school today."

"Sounds like her," I say, "Why don't you two try and go back to bed."

They both run back up the stairs giggling like the two kids they are. I go on to the basement to settle things with Sarah.

She didn't turn on the lights, so it's still dark. "Sorry you have to stay down here all day."

"It's fine; it'll give me some more time to sleep."

"Uh, quick question," I stutter, "When are you going to need blood and all?"

"I think I can make it another few days without it."

I slide my hand around the wall to turn on the light. The light clicks on and I see her curled up in one of the chairs.

"There should be a cot somewhere down here," I tell her, searching one of the shelves. I pull one out and start setting it up in front of the table. She's still trembling despite the two days of rest she's had.

The front door upstairs opens up and I hear the familiar sound of my wife's keys jingling as she walks in. "Honey!" she shouts, "I saw your truck, are you home already?"

I smash my head into the doorway, "Yes, I came back for something important!"

"What is it?" She asks, walking down the stairs coming into full view of Sarah, "Who's this?"

"She's why," I reply, circling her arm and pulling her back up the stairs.

She pushes me away midway up the stairs, "What the hell? Who is that?"

"Complicated answer—"

"I swear; you better make it simple."

"Uh—"

She storms off into the kitchen and appears to start making food. "I just need to sit you down and explain this."

She stirs the flour in silence as I walk over to the kitchen. Right as my footsteps over the tile line, she pulls the whisk on me.

"I swear to whatever higher being there is that if you're cheating on me with a fifteen-year-old girl, I will kill you with this whisk."

"That's not it," I explain, "not at all. I just need to sit you down and tell you what's going on."

She puts the whisk back in the bowl and starts stirring up the eggs. "Explain. Right here, right now."

I look to the stairs to see if the girls are listening in. "She's a homeless girl that was living with my grandpa."

She stops stirring and looks up at me. "You're grandpa has been dead for a month."

"She's been living there for a while—"

"So what? She's been living with without anybody knowing for who knows how long?"

I take a deep breath and think of ways to tell it how it is.

"I was living with Abe for fifteen years," I hear Sarah say, standing in the doorway of the basement, bound by the sun streak shining on the ground.

"Who the hell is Abe?" my wife retorts.

"His grandfather, that's what I've always called him."

"You really expect me to believe that he was raising a newborn for the last fifteen years without any of us knowing?"

"That's the complicated part," Sarah replies.

⊲⊦ ⊙ ⊦⊳

"A goddamn vampire?" Linda shouts. She rushes to one of the cabinets and pulls out a small box.

"What's that?" I ask.

She pulls out a drug testing strip from the box and holds it in front of me. "Linda, why do you have drug tests?"

"I know who I married. Open up," she tells me as she puts it in my mouth. A moment later she runs it under the tap water, showing up negative.

"Do you have any idea how ridiculous you sound?" she says aloud, bending over the sink with her hand over her face.

The doorbell rings and I rush to my feet to avoid continuing this conversation. Sarah moves down into the dark, artificially lit basement while I go to answer the door.

I open the door and a familiar-looking youngster presents himself to me, basically covered from head to toe with his hood up and sunglasses this early in the morning.

"Can I help you?"

"Yeah, my little sister is missing, so I've been going door to door asking if anyone's seen her," he tells me. His voice is insincere. I reach over to grab Grandpa's big UV flashlight sitting on my bags across from me.

"Who's there?" Linda asks from the kitchen, but I ignore her.

I flash the light into his face to make sure he's an actual person, but the young man just covers it with his bare hands. "Sir, I'm looking for my sister, if you don't have anything to provide for me," he rambles on, "You can just ask me to leave."

It finally strikes me; this young man is the one who was following us on the way back to town. I turn off the light and he slips his hand back into his coat jacket. His nostrils flare a few times as he seems to be sniffing something.

He leans over closer to me. "I know she's here. If I need to make it look like another hunting accident, I will."

Things start making more and more sense and he is the missing piece of logic in this whole mess. I bite my lip in self-control and flip on the light directly into his face.

Without flinching, his face starts to turn red with the vessels beneath the skin starting to make their way to the surface. "If that's how you'd rather make it," he replies, turning and walking away.

"The hell?" Linda says, closing the door and snatching the light away from my hand, "Who was that and why were you shining this into his face?"

"It's nobody, Linda," I tell her, "Can you take the girls to school today?"

"I was planning on it anyway." She turns off the light and walks back into the kitchen to finish the kids' breakfast. I begin to hear the skittering of the girls' feet above the ceiling as they go about getting ready for their day.

I walk over behind my wife and lean close to her. "This girl is in serious danger, Linda. Please trust me on this."

"And what? I'm just supposed to accept the fact that she's a mythical creature that doesn't exist."

"I saw her catch a bird with her bare hands and eat it; she could probably lift a car."

"If she's in so much danger, then why didn't you call the police—"

"I was in the middle of nowhere, and I was counting that you'd be able to help me deal with this."

She looks at me in the eyes, and tells me, "Why should I believe any of this?"

The girls come down the stairs, saving me from this debate with Linda. Two of them rush to their mother's side, while Julie grabs the plate of pancakes and goes to the other room to eat them.

"Are you *one-two—*, Julie, where are you? Are all of you ready for school?" she looks for the final child.

"Yeah!" Julie shouts from the other room with a mouth full of food.

"I'll take them to school, you—" Linda pauses, "Just deal with her."

"I will," I reply, hugging two of our daughters and going in to kiss my wife.

She puts her hand between our faces. "I'm seriously pissed about this; we'll figure this out when I get home from work."

She leads the kids into the other room to eat their breakfast. Despite her anger, she did leave me a plate of food. I look over to see Julie with her stack of pancakes twice as high as her sisters'.

I take the pancakes she left me and walk down into the basement to give them to Sarah. I haven't seen her eat regular food for a while. "Sarah?" I call her, coming down to a dark room.

I flip on the light to see her curled up on the chair, clenching her hands on her legs. "You alright?" I ask.

She's trembling more than before, but a moment later, she looks up at me. "There was another vampire here," she says.

"How'd you know?" I ask.

"I could smell him," she explains, "And I know who it is; he's the one that's been hunting me this whole time.

"He's the face I remember most clearly from savage life. I don't want to go back."

She buries her face into her knees and begins sobbing. I set the food on the table beside and set my hand on her head. "We'll figure this out, kid. Just give it time.

"Eat the food, get some rest; the sun's out," I tell her. I go back up the stairs and close the door. I scan the room and realize how dirty it's been and how busy my wife must've been lately. And with that, I begin cleaning and putting the kids' toys away.

Time goes about and I lose myself in work. My wife comes in through the front door and drops her keys in the dish beside the door.

"Hey, honey!" I shout across the house with no response.

She makes her way into the room where I'm cleaning. "Can you just take her somewhere for a bit so I don't have to share the house with a strange teenager?"

"Yes, honey," I concede, "I'll have to wait until sunset though."

"Whatever. Just give it twenty minutes." She turns away and walks up the stairs, leaving me to the cleaning. The sun begins to set signaling me to put away all the cleaning chemicals before the kids come back home.

◂◉▸

We pull back up to the house coming home from taking Sarah to the local park for a small mammal. She's sitting there with her face in her hands. "You alright?"

"I just hate that I'm forced to do what I do," she tells me, "Abe made it easy with his hunting habits."

"Are you at least feeling less jittery?"

"It'll take some time for me."

We get out of the car to head back into the house. I notice a car I don't recognize in the driveway; old and beat up with splotches of blue paint. I look back at Sarah who's staring up at the lack of stars from the city lights.

I make my way to the door and unlock it, slightly eager to see who's new to the house, slightly discouraged by the quality of the car.

The door opens and I'm greeted with the punk from earlier. I drop my keys to the floor and reach for Grandpa's flashlight I left by the door, but my fingers only feel the magazines sitting there.

"Oh honey," my wife says through her teeth, "This young man is looking for his sister, he got word she was with you."

The man stands up and kicks the sofa to the side. My wife screams and the children run up to their rooms. "You're here now, This'll be entertaining."

I prep my fists and march towards him, ready to fight, but he just grabs me by the arm and tosses me behind him across the house. I crash headfirst into some vases, and my wife screams bloody murder, running to my side.

"I'll feed off you later, I'm here for someone else," he says, walking toward the front door. It bursts open with Sarah running so fast towards him. I get back on my feet, and push my wife behind me as she's frightened beyond her wits.

Faster than I can distinguish, they throw punches at each other. Eventually, the man grabs Sarah by the head, digging what seems like claws into her skin. She screams in pain while he makes her bow. Blood flows down her face from the wounds.

I see her eyes flutter like they did back at the estate, and her fingers sprout long pointed nails. She swipes them across his lower jaw, slicing into his face and upper neck making him let go. She claws one after another, trading blows, drawing more and more blood spraying across the house.

My wife grabs the kitchen phone starts dialing for somebody as I move to keep her behind me.

"Hello? Police?" she frantically talks into the phone. I hear the operator calmly repeat their greeting.

"There are literally two monsters fighting to the death in my house—"

I overhear the speaker from the phone say, "Ma'am monsters don't exist."

She starts to scream into the phone. "Someone is going to be killed; I need damn cops right now!"

The man grabs her by the throat, but not for a killing blow, but throws her into the kitchen table. All the plates and decoration crash to the ground along with the chairs and the table itself are crushed by the impact. My wife screams again in shock and repeats our home address to the operator.

"You're coming back with me whether you want to or not," the man says to Sarah, "This isn't about choice here."

I see her hand reaching for a broken part of the chair. "You mean to stake me?" he asks.

One moment it's in her hand, and the next she's already thrown it directly at his heart, but he catches it firmly in his hand. She screams in anger and launches herself towards him, grabbing the chair piece and stabbing it through his chest. She exerts even more, pushing him to the wall to the left of the front window like a thumbtack.

My wife is caught off guard and drops the phone, yanking it from the wall. I look over to see two of the girls watching intently in between the stairs and the ceiling.

In the mirror, I see Sarah sprouting fangs in front of her canines and her eyes growing wide. The man spreads some of his own blood on his hands and just looks at it. "And here, I thought you'd grown weak in fifteen years," he says, wiping his blood on her face, "Let's really check that."

Her tongue brushes her lips and her hands begin to shake, slowly moving up towards his face. Her mouth begins to open and move towards his throat.

"Sarah!" I shout to her, "Think about what you're doing."

She stops immediately and freezes with intense conflict in her eyes. The man whispers something to her, and she bites directly into her lips.

"Sarah!" I shout again, slowly moving towards them, but my wife grabs my arm.

"Don't you dare," my wife says.

Sarah slowly backs away, looking dazed after her fight. She shakes her head and says, "I'm not going back."

The man, staked to my wall covered in blood and lacerations, starts to laugh. "I won't be the last one," he says, laughing. His laughing comes to an abrupt stop when he coughs some blood and falls limp.

Sarah falls into the chair that was kicked out of the way earlier and starts to dig her claws into the arms of the couch. Her jaws clenched and she closes her eyes.

"What the hell?" my wife says to break the silence, "There actually are vampires that exist."

I walk over to Sarah, trying to think of what to say. "Go get cleaned up before the police come."

The wounds on her face slowly close up and hide themselves under the blood splattered on her face. She lifts her fingers and the sharp nails fall off, revealing normal-looking fingertips.

Tears flow down her face for who knows what, and she wipes away the blood on her face. She nods and says, "Yeah, I'll do that."

❮❙ ⦿ ❙❯

Red and blue lights start lighting up the outside, followed by a large, burly overweight policeman walking through our door with a gun in hand.

"Hello?" he barks, "Anyone here?"

He makes it through the doorway and looks right upon the dead body hanging on the wall. "Crap," he says, putting down the gun and signaling the other officers, "Get a body bag!"

The family, including Sarah, is all cuddled in the kitchen. I walk out to the officer, and everyone slowly comes into view.

"Hey officer," I say, "Uh, so—"

He pulls out a notepad and starts writing, "So what you're telling me two very high, very dangerous nondescript persons broke into your house and began to quarrel. You and your family of, uh, six felt endangered, fled to a safer area until this fell silent.

"When you came to the current scene, one of the very high, very dangerous, nondescript persons fled the scene."

He finishes writing and clicks his pen. "No, I did not leave anything out."

"Um, what?" I ask him, confused about that whole ramble.

He pulls me aside by the arm and whispers, "Look, I hate dealing with these types of cases, so just let it be."

He looks around at the wrecked house, and waves his hand for the other officers to start their work. He looks at my family; my three daughters huddle behind their mother, and Sarah standing off to the side. He, what I think, sniffs a few times and stares down Sarah, whose hair is still wet from the shower.

"You," he says pointing at Sarah, "Stay out of trouble."

He turns back to me and hands me a torn piece of paper. "If you need anything related to this situation, call this number and ask for the name written on the paper."

I start smoothing out the bubbles on the window vinyl. The pamphlet said this is stronger than SPF five-hundred, but it's probably just advertising nonsense.

That policeman happened to also be clued in on the existence of vampires, and is very empathetic towards those like Sarah; he offered new documents for her and showed us modern amenities to normalize her life.

The sun begins peeking from behind the horizon and starts shining through the vinyl covered windows, casting light on the wall. Sarah slowly reaches her hands into the light.

"I haven't seen the sunrise in over fifteen years," she tells us through tears, "It's weird, you know?"

"The officer also pointed us to some special sunscreen if you ever need to go outside," I tell her, pointing to the box full of cream in the corner.

She wipes away her tears. "I don't think I'll be ready for that quite yet."

Julie walks up and hugs her leg. "Can we have breakfast yet?" Julie cries, with Sarah resting her hand on her head.

Immortal Minds

⊷◎⊶

I LOOK OUT into the rain, contemplating what's left of my brothers and sisters. There're only two of us left; there used to be one-hundred-fifty. Slowly, over the millennia, we've been hunted down and murdered. My mind is filled with the thoughts of my last brother; it used to be overwhelming with so many voices; it was for all of us. But we've dwindled down to just us two survivors.

"They've found me," I hear my brother think. I stand up and focus on his voice.

"What do you mean?" I ask back.

"They've been following me for the past two blocks."

"Are you sure it's them?"

"Who else would be following me?" he tells me, "Are you safe?"

"I've been hiding in the woods for the past months, moving further and further out."

"I'm positive it's them, I'm going to have to fight them off."

"Be safe, brother," I think, "I'll be right here waiting for you."

◁‖ ⊙ ‖▷

Humanity has always hated us; they blamed us for all catastrophes throughout time. Whenever we're in proximity to each other, disaster strikes. We've tried to live together, separated from the rest of humanity, but they hunted us despite our efforts.

When humanity became hateful towards us, we dispersed across the world. But they hunted us down still, one by one.

"I've been captured," he tells me, after hours of silence.

"Can you get out?" I ask.

"I don't think so."

I sit back down and begin to cry. He's half a world away, and I'm unable to do anything but hear his dying thoughts.

"Alice," I hear him think, "I love you, but this is it."

"No," I think, curling up in my tears, "Don't go."

I hear him sing a song in his head, my favorite of the ancient songs we would sing as a tribe. He would pause and pick back up again periodically in his head. I couldn't bear to think of what they were doing to him.

As he finished his song, I feel his grasp slip away. This is it. My mind is silent save it only be my thoughts; I'm the only one left, I'm completely alone.

The silence is deafening, I can't hear anyone anymore. I only hear the birds and the wind blowing around. All I can do is sit here and cry alone. I begin to sing songs of my people; my extinct people.

Into The Wildlands

❮❯◎❮❯

"GOOD MORNING, class," our teacher says, starting the class for the day. In unison, we repeat, "Good morning, instructor."

We sit down and begin our daily learning, as we do every day. We review our history, the same history we reviewed yesterday and the day before. Mathematics and roles in society we'll eventually fill when we reach a certain age.

I wonder if I'm alone in what I think, that this is a waste of time. I long for something better, something that feels more fulfilling than school and the eventual jobs we'll work until the day we die.

I raise my hand to ask a question about the working class. I hear my teacher pause, breathe in and out. "Yes, Scott?"

"What if I don't want to work the jobs I'm assigned," I ask.

Our teacher walks up to my desk, raises his hand and backhands me. I sit back up with the taste of blood in my mouth as he walks back to the front of the room to continue the lesson. As if nothing had happened, we continue on society's social and economic structure.

The class goes on until it's almost leisure time. Right before the clock ticks the time, our teacher ends by saying, "Any questions, Scott?"

"No sir," I reply.

"Good, then you are all dismissed."

In unison, the class stands up and walks out in a single file. Jennifer is always two people ahead of me in line. She's a good friend I've had for many years. She cares for me like no other. All the people around me are always so cold and collective, but she has always been different.

The door to outside slides open as my classmates scan their ID tags. One by one we all make it outside. Jennifer scans hers and walk outside, but begins meandering a mysterious pattern, curving in an oddly specific path.

I scan mine and walk outside to her. She grabs my arm and starts pulling me along this path. "What are you doing?" I laugh.

"The cameras can't see us right now," she explains, "Are you okay?"

"Yeah, I'm okay," I tell her.

"You need to stop breaking the rules. You know what they do to rule breakers like you, right?"

"Dumb jobs, bad living conditions, etcetera," I say, "Probably."

She stops and looks at me, "And I don't want that to happen to you, Scott."

I smile, "Thanks, but I'll be okay. No need to worry."

⇇ ⊙ ⇉

Class goes just as it did yesterday. Reviewing history, mathematics, and the other subjects I've studied for my whole life. We begin to talk about the structure of the walls we live in. Osheky live in the center, surrounded by normal people, with the Savage and the Wildlands outside of the walls. Nothing I haven't been taught hundreds of times before.

Something unusual today. One of the Osheky walks into our classroom. The teacher falls silent in awe but swiftly bows as per law. I look around to see the entire class facing down at their desks. I look back at the teacher and partially lower my head, but just enough for me to see what the Osheky is going to do.

This is the first time I've seen an Osheky in person. He's almost as tall as the doorway, dressed in loose beige clothes with the signature pastel white painted skin with a single, bright red circle painted across his entire face. Silently, he looks around and we lock eyes.

"What a pleasure—," our teacher attempts to say, before being slapped by the Osheky. I hear something crack right before he's slammed into the chalkboard. I guess Osheky are as strong as they say.

The Osheky waves his hand under the hand sanitizer and walks out of the classroom. The teacher claws his way back to his feet and signals Ashley to talk over the intercom for him. She walks up and presses the button and says, "Instructor for room 18 requires medical assistance, please."

The intercom speaks back, "Yes, thank you. Walk him over to the nurses."

A few of the other students Ashley chose carried him outside the classroom. As per rule, we all remain silent and work on classwork, but I sit there, think about the magnificence of that Osheky man.

Not long after, it's leisure time, and we walk out a single file to the outside. I'm still struck by that Osheky after all day.

◄╫ ⊙ ╫►

Mr. Otto didn't come back to teach for months, on most days we had another teacher come and teach the same boring material I've already learned. Some other days we were left alone to ourselves.

When Mr. Otto did return, it was almost time for us to be assigned to the working class in society. After classes stopped, we spent a lot of time, being interviewed, evaluated, and tested for our working positions.

When my class was finished being evaluated, we simply went back to classes, going over the same boring history, the same boring math and curriculum.

"Scott, can you recall the purpose of the outer wall?" Mr. Otto asks me, bringing me out of my haze. He sounds different after his medical leave.

"To maintain the safety between us and the Wildlands and the savages that live there," I repeat.

"Good, Now what's the purpose of the inner wall?" he asks.

"To separate us from Osheky—"

"That's incorrect," he interrupts me, knowing I'm right, "You would know the correct answer if you paying attention.

"One day, you'll regret your insubordination."

The intercom begins to speak over him, "Please send Scott to room 2, immediately."

Mr. Otto stares me down, and the class glances in my direction as I stand up and leave. Room 2 is an administration room, and this no doubt has something to do with our working assessments.

"Scott reporting to room 2," I tell the door.

The door opens, and I'm greeted by Madam Grenand, one of the highest-ranking officials in the government. "Hello Scott, please come in."

I stand there in shock, speechless. Why would she of all people call me in? "Lost for words?" she asks, pulling me in by my sleeve.

"Good morning, Madam Grenand," I finally said, sitting down at one side of the table.

"Good morning, Scott," she says, putting a thick folder full of paper in front of me, "Do you know what's in that folder?"

"I don't, madam."

"Go ahead and open it and find out."

I lift the folder revealing its contents; I read the first page and it's a report on me, from when I was a child. I move to the next one, and it's a similar report.

"We take insubordination very seriously." I flip through the rest of the papers, and it's just report after report about me and the things I've done out of line.

She drops another folder, and I begin to move through it. It's Jennifer's folder, full of reports of her own. "I'll save you the time of reading those, but *every* single one of her pertains to you in some form.

"So I'm here to strike a deal."

⫷ ⊙ ⫸

"We keep files like this for *everyone*, for all sorts of things, including insubordination," She tells me, "We know you care for Jennifer very much, and we would like her to progress forward without impedance from you.

"So, here's the deal: you take full accountability and punishment of both of yours' insubordination, and she goes on to her full potential."

"What if I say no?" I ask.

"Even now, questioning every little thing," she remarks, "You say no, we're forced to punish both of you, impeding her progress."

I look at her most recent report, avoiding surveillance and unpermitted physical contact. "I don't think I have many choices here."

"Good, good. Keep that up."

⊰⊙⊱

I've been assigned to garbage collection in the outer rim. Everyone is restricted from conversing with each other, just day in and day out, disposing of the collective waste of the less developed outer rim of the city. This is the closest I've ever been to a wall, just not the wall I wanted to see.

Everyday, the same thing: Collect waste, inspect the wall. On occasion, I hear strange noises from beyond the wall I've never heard before. Jennifer and I were restricted from communicating too often. In the end, it was my choices and my consequences that put me here. Frankly, I don't regret it.

Today is just another day on the route. I hop off the back of the truck and grab the bucket of garbage. As I set the bucket back down, and I'm suddenly greeted by an Osheky man. I stand there in shock, intimidated even as the others working with me bow and cover their eyes.

I stumble back, resting against the truck. It says something in its language, but I barely understand. Its voice is deep, its power piercing through my bones. "You are brave," I think it says.

It begins to walk away, but I wonder why an Osheky would be this far into the outer ring. I'm left admiring the magnificence and power he exudes. One of my coworkers slaps my chest and we continue on with our job, but I'm still pondering the Osheky.

⊣⊢ ⊙ ⊢⊣

Yet another day of work. Typing on computer day after day with no end in sight. Copying documents is all I do nowadays, but at least I get to read some interesting stuff that I'm not allowed to share to a single soul. Ranging from handwritten civil reports, to censored Osheky research.

The sounds of all the typists can be a bit much at times, hundreds of us working at all hours of the day. Some of the others begin gasping, and the room steadily becomes quieter and quieter, but I keep working as I'm told. Finally the room falls silent, and I look up to see why. The magnificent Osheky have arrived; I bow my head and cover my eyes as protocol.

One of the authorities begins to talk to him in their language. "Hello, what do I owe the pleasure—"

I hear a thud and the Osheky man correcting him in what to say. It begins to walk, but I don't know where and I hear it call out, "Jennifer, ninety-one forty-two."

Fear strikes me, why would they be calling for me? What on earth would they want from me?

As per protocol, but shaking with fear, I begin to move to my feet. I stand up, looking straight at the pastel white painted with bright, blood-red runes into their face. I offer a formal greeting, but I'm shaken to the core with its immeasurable dominance and strength.

It walks up to me, staring me down from its towering body. Slowly, step after harrowing step it approaches me and now I am face to face with the superior life form.

The Osheky tilts its head, "Jennifer?" My mind speaks, but my mouth shivers. "There's no need to be afraid," he says, "I have a favor to ask you."

I look behind him to see a government official glaring back at me. I look back at the Osheky man. "I need you, Jennifer, to escort me to the outer ring in a few days."

"Omuro, please, we can personally escort you to wherever you—"

He grabs her by the throat and lifts her to eye level. "You insignificant human, you will address me as you should. Don't be complacent.

"I will have this woman escort me as I choose." he tosses her aside and storms out.

◄╫ ⊙ ╫►

"Background check came clean, Madam Grenand," I hear, "Everything that's already on her file has been reviewed already."

"Then why is Omuru, the second highest-ranking Osheky," she says before shouting at the top of her lungs, "Requesting this woman!"

I'm trembling in my shoes, chained to a table; I don't know what to do.

"Pull Omuro's file," she says before walking through the door with two men in black with strange contraptions in their hands.

"H-hello, Madam Gre-," I attempt to greet her.

"Cut the crap Jennifer," she says. I've never heard anyone talk like that, so casually, much less a government official. "How do you know Omuro? You've never been cleared to interact with any Osheky."

She fuming out her ears, she's so angry. I stutter my words, "I- I've never met him."

I start crying as I've never done before. Another man comes through the door. "Omuro's file came clean of anything related to Jennifer, Madam."

"That's impossible," she whispers to him, "I'll review it myself."

"His file spans for more than eighty years, Madam—"

"I didn't stutter," she grits her teeth, "Jennifer, stop crying. We'll prepare you for his escort."

◀◎▶

Another day goes by of work. I can't even keep track of the days anymore, they all blend together. I toss the bin full of garbage into the truck, but I accidentally throw it all against the side instead.

"Crap!" I shout aloud, as I begin to clean up the mess. My coworkers shake their heads and try to keep busy as I work my way.

I look around to admire whatever scenery I can. Today we're driving past a bare section of the outer wall. I turn around and come face to face with the Osheky man I frequently see here. I jump back in surprise, hit the truck, and go into full panic.

He leans over to my ear and begins to whisper, "Leave with us."

"W-what do you mean?" I say, trying to keep my legs from turning to jelly. He walks to the front of the truck and kicks the entire truck out of the way. His leg leaves the whole section of the vehicle completely crushed. At first, all I see is my coworkers freaking out trying to not fall out of the truck, but then I see someone I thought I'd never see again.

Jennifer screams as the truck slides past her and nearly falls over. I look back at the Osheky man as he presses something in his hands, and the wall explodes.

"What are you doing?" Jennifer yells through her tears of fear. The smoke clears and reveals the Wildlands; lush with trees and little creatures I've never seen before, fleeing from us.

"Now's your chance, boy!" He laughs, walking backward to his freedom, "Come if you want, but I chose you, so don't let me down!"

He makes his way, one step after another to freedom; freedom from all this. I hear my coworkers running away, back into civilization.

Something deep inside grabs ahold of me, and I take a step towards the Wildlands. I take another, and another, until I'm running to my freedom. But I stop before I step beyond the wall and look back at Jennifer, who's crying in a crouched position. I see her mouth moving as she mutters something to herself.

"Jennifer!" I shout, "Come on, this is our chance!"

She looks at me, ready to leave forever. I run to her and I hear her say, "You don't understand, they'll find you out there. They're already coming."

"What do you mean, Jennifer? Come on, we can leave."

"Omuro's been being followed this whole time, they're not going to let you leave."

"Come on, aren't you coming?" the Osheky man shouts, "This is never going to happen again for you!"

I grab hold of her hand and bring her to her feet.

⊶ ⊙ ⊷

I guide her to the freedom I never knew I'd dreamt about. Slowly she begins to walk with me to the Wildlands. We reach the unkept dirt and trees on the outside when she pulls away. I lose my balance and fall down a slope.

The Osheky catches me and lifts me up with a single hand. "Jennifer!" I call out.

"No, I can't," she says, "I can't go with you."

She breaks down into full out tears. "Remember me—" She says before a loud bang and a spray of blood knocks her down.

I try to rush back to her, about to climb the slope back up but he grabs on to me again. "Think very clearly about that choice. You go back up there, and you're not coming back.

"You either go to her with no guarantee of being with her or come with me for freedom."

He lets go of me and Jennifer begins to stand back up with a hole through her shoulder. She's weak, but braces up against the wall to stand.

She smiles at for what seems to be the last time as I run back to her. Another loud bang and she falls once again. I hear something travel past my ear. Some instinct deep down inside takes hold and I begin to run; run away from her in fear.

The Osheky man and I run into the dense landscape until the last light of civilization disappears. Tears flow down my face as I slowly realize what I've actually done.

After a while the trees become more dispersed and I begin to see shadows moving across us. The shadows turn into people running with us. I trip and fall hard into the dirt, when I look back up I see about twenty other people, but they all look so strange, but strangest of all is water.

I look around to see water extending across the landscape, and it seems to move. I'm lifted up by the Osheky and set inside a huge wooden capsule.

"What's going on?" I ask, descending into panic.

He laughs, "You have a lot to learn, but for now, we make our escape."

Life After War

⫷◎⫸

I REMEMBER EACH and every day; every surgery, abuse, and all the pain. It was solyear 2662. Collestrisian Dictator Frederick deWalter was finally overthrown after twelve gruelling and utterly agonizing solyears. He was a madman; speaking about a prophecy from God all the time. He was a serpent with a silver tongue and rallied behind economic salvation. And hundreds of millions believed him as if it had never been done before.

Even he had his pride and joy, the future of mankind, perfect soldiers of every kind. All that started with sixty-six handpicked newborn baby girls, one of them have the unfortunate opportunity to be me. Twelve of us did not survive the twelve years of experimentation, suffering and torture. Our bodies were forced to grow at an accelerated rate; as a result our bones became severely bowed and warped as our organs reached near adult size. One by one, our bones were broken, reshaped, and reinforced with titanium alloys over years of repetitive abuse and surgery.

Alongside this agony was another; our muscles were rewoven with electrically conductive fibers connected to sixteen probes on our backs so we could be painfully forced, against our will, to be experimented on. Our muscles would be torn to shreds, rebuilt, and started again from our toes to our fingers over and over again.

We were chemically treated in every way imaginable, from ingestion to intravenous; our stomachs would be pumped with strange substances to see how the reaction would proceed inside a human being. From chemical A to triple-Z, we were nothing but animal test subjects for his regime.

Twelve solyears from birth, this was every moment of our lives and we knew not the better. The fifty-four of us who survived were thrown into a whole new foreign world that was more than a torture dungeon where unspeakable horrors and experiments were performed. It took a total of two solyears for all 48 of us to be rehabilitated into the Martian society, the other six couldn't adapt and had to be sent to psychiatric wards permanently. We learned to read, write and basic mathematics in record time and we were all sent to families and private schools for constant supervision. The United States military was able to track down a few of the biological parents, including someone who claimed to be my father.

My supposed father took me to humanity's homeworld of Earth, where I attended public school in Southern Utah. You could pick me out in any crowd; I stuck out like a tree in grassy plains. I was one of six who fled Mars, one other who came to Earth, three fled to Venus, and the last two became vagrants wandering around the solar system.

Years go by, but there's not a single day where I don't feel the agony of all those years. With a turn of good luck, I made many new friends after I started public school, but there are bad people wherever you go.

◄◄ ⊙ ►►

Some girl marches up to me and slams my locker shut right on my arm, metal clashing metal. She's been stalking me ever since I showed up. "Bet that hurt, huh?" she asks.

"No," I reply. Her face wrinkles in anger and she flicks the metal plate in my forehead.

"What the hell?" she grabs her finger in pain, cradling her hand, "You freak! You illegal alien!"

She shoves me into the wall and swaggers away. Godrick comes up to me and ruffles my hair. "You know I don't like it when you do that," I tell him.

"I'm impressed that all the crap you take from people doesn't affect you," he replies, "How was class?"

"I finished all the books already. My father wants them to move me up a grade, but they don't want to."

"Well, what do you want?"

"I mean, this is all fine." The bell rings and then a hoard of other kids migrate to one end of the hallway or the other. We, like every other day we see each other, walk together to our adjacent classes.

"So, uh, there's a great movie on Saturday—"

"And, you want me to go with you?" I interrupt him.

"I mean, yeah preferably, but I think you just need to get out more," he says, bumping into me, "I never hear about you doing anything fun."

"Well, that's because I don't."

I head off into my classroom for my final class of the day: English. It's nothing but reading books and writing essays, and that school bully happens to share that class with me.

◄◄ ⊙ ►►

I close the door behind me and toss my house keys on the counter. The bowl rings and wobbles a little. "Dad, I'm home!"

"Hey Milly!" he shouts from the other room, "How was school?"

"Same as every other day," I reply.

I walk into the bathroom to see how I look. "Hey dad, is it alright if I go out to the movies on Saturday?"

I hear him spit out his drink and rush around the corner. "Since when do you want to go to the movies? Or anywhere for that matter?"

"Well, can I go or not?" I persist.

"I mean, yeah of course."

I stretch my arms up to uncatch my bra off a probe on my back. I look at my bright white hair and how I might style it. "There isn't a boy involved, is there?"

"I mean, I'm going with friends—" he snorts and laughs a little.

"Nothing like a little romance to get you out of the house," he retorts. I glare back at him in annoyance. "I'm kidding, I'm kidding. I'm just glad you're finally getting out," he says.

⊷ ⊙ ⊶

"What movie is this again?" I ask Godrick.

"It's a rerun of Star Wars: The Old Republic," he informs me.

"What's it about?" I ask.

He whips around and starts to walk backward, "How do you not know what it's about? It's been out for fifty years."

"We can say I didn't get out much."

He trips a little and runs into the door to the theater. "Excuse me, but here we are m'lady," he says while opening the door, which is apparently something men are supposed to do. My English class is having me read older literature from 1950 to 2050 and the decline of chivalry.

"So, I'm going to run you down, Star Wars has been around since 1970 or whatever, it's about a guy named Luke—"

"I'm going to stop you right there Godrick, let's just watch the movie, I don't need a multi-century rundown."

"Agh, come on," he walks me to the cashier, "Two tickets, please. Can you at least act a little excited?"

"If the movie's been out for fifty years, couldn't you just have watched it at home?"

We walk into the theater room, and I see for the first time a huge white screen used solely for entertainment. Oddly curious, but unpleasant nonetheless. "Well, I obviously didn't get to see the original theater release."

We sit down in allegedly in the best seats in the entire theater. "And on top of that, it's freakin' IMAX!" he shouts, ploping down on the chair.

"Cool, Godrick," I tell him, slowly sitting down and moving my coat to get comfortable, "But why bring me?"

"Never once have I ever even heard of you having fun or going out, or doing literally anything; I see you at school reading some paper books and that's it!"

The lights dim and the bright lights of the projector begin shining in the dark. The movie starts, which is apparently when advertisements play preceding the actual movie. Also also, I do not enjoy Star Wars.

Something about fictional people with telekinesis and laser swords, when Godrick slides his hand under mine; I feel a strange sensation throughout my abdomen, something different than active electrical running through my muscles or intravenous chemicals.

I slowly squeeze my hand in return and the feeling gets stronger, I feel queasy and warm. I look over to Godrick to see his skin bright red under the projector light.

⊲⊹ ⊙ ⊹⊳

"So, Milly, how was the movie?" Jill asks, rushing up beside me.

"It was okay, can't say I'm interested in Star Wars," I tell her. She bumps my arm repeatedly as we walk into the school.

"Is there anything else that happened?" she persists.

"Is there something you want to hear?" Jill rolls her eyes and sighs. We join the crowd as we funnel through the doors.

"You know that Godrick wants you, right?" she bursts out.

"I'm probably misinterpreting that question."

She grunts and stops me in my steps. "He's been trying really hard to be subtle about it, and I heard that he grabbed your hand during the movie."

"Yeah? What about it?" I ask.

"Milly, do you have any clue what that means?"

"No," I confess. Social interactions for me are mysterious since I grew up isolated on Mars with sixty-six other girls, whom I was tortured with. During rehab, we spent a lot of time on social, but I've never been able to apply any of that.

"He's head over heels for you," she stares me down and pauses for me to be confused. "He's in love with you Milly!"

This catches me by surprise, and I freeze, like a clock with gears that are bound up. This is something new; I utter the word, "What?"

"Everyone around us has seen it, there have been rumors ever since you arrived," she explains.

"I didn't really know," I say, as the wheels start turning again. My face gets warm, but I don't remember what this feeling is called, "I-I, uh —"

"You should maybe read some books on psychology, Milly."

"I-I, uh—"

Jill grunts in disappointment and runs off into the crowd to get to class.

⁕ ⊙ ⁕

Godrick walks up behind; I feel his hand slide across my back, but his fingernail catches on one of my probes. He jumps back and screams in pain.

"Ow!" we both scream, "Watch out for those, Godrick!"

He shakes his hand about trying to ease his pain, "Well, sorry! It's not like I can see them."

I lean over and kiss his cheek and he starts walking back to class. "How's class?" I ask interlocking his hand into mine.

"Fine, you know, just stupid precalc," he goes off, "Stupid derivatives and trig. Unlike you, I don't get to skip a grade." He leans over and kisses me back. The rest of our walk to his class is in silence. Jill bumps me in the hip as she walks by.

"You remember when I spilled the tea on Godrick and you turned red as a tomato?" she starts laughing, "Ha, look at you now."

"Ha ha," I sarcastically slow laugh as she rushes away. As I go about to open the door to go into class, something hits me in the head.

I look down at a slightly bruised and browned apple. I look away to where it came from only to see Berkeley, the school bully raising both her middle fingers at me. I disregard her and walk into class. She's had it out for me ever since I moved to Earth.

Life here is surprisingly local; interplanetary news is always on the television, but in the day to day, it's never important. Mars this, Venus that, man colonizes another of Jupiter's moons.

This past year as we get closer to graduation she's become increasingly aggressive and borderline violent. I went to a teacher, but they informed me that her she was the niece of a county secretary and that no one really cared.

I continue off into class, where I go about my usual routine of reading and homework and ignoring the world around me. Before I know it class is over and I'm off back home.

"Dad, I'm home!" I shout, tossing my keys into the metal bowl. I breathe in a strange scent I don't get to indulge in very often: cake.

"Why are you baking?" I shout again.

"Graduation is tomorrow, isn't it?" he yells.

"No, Dad, it's next week," I reply walking into the kitchen, "That smells great though."

"Crap, I was so excited, too," he sets down the pan with a golden brown cake, "So about your graduation party—"

"Dad, please, I don't want one."

"But you have not once hosted a party."

"I don't want one and that's final."

He turns to me with big eyes, "Can you at least go out with your friends, this is a once in a lifetime—"

"Fine..."

◀▮ ⊙ ▮▶

As we kiss, he starts to slide his hand up the back of my shirt. I feel passion, but it all stops when he touches a probe and simply stops. "What is it now, Godrick?" I'm annoyed, everytime we try this, it never goes anywhere. This is where it always stops.

"I can't do it, Milly," he says, backing up and tucking his shirt back in, "You need to tell me about all that; you need to tell me about before you arrived on Earth. I barely know anything about you except anything that's happened since you moved to Utah."

I roll my eyes and fall back on the bed. "Why do you need to know, Godrick. It's the past, the past is supposed to be buried."

"It's not healthy to bury your issues, and you know that."

"Let's just go out, please, I don't want to go over this again," I say, zipping my pants and making myself decent for the public.

He sighs, and I know that sigh; he yearns to know my past, but he doesn't want to argue. He slides on his jacket and follows behind me.

"Okay," he says, "Let's go to Jerry's."

"Godrick, I don't want to drink—"

"How do you know that? You've never gotten drunk, you should try it."

"Godrick, I don't want to."

"Milly, you're twenty-two and you've never even had a drink."

"If I go get drunk and go home, are you going to drop this?" I ask. The rain starts coming down as we walk down the sidewalk.

"Yes, I promise," he replies, "Pinky-promise."

We walk all the way to Jerry's and Godrick decides to make an entrance into the bar. "Bartender! She wants to get drunk!"

"Godrick!" I chastise him, punching him in the arm.

"Ah!" he responds. I may have punched him too hard. I look down the bar only to see Berkeley sitting at the very end; she glances over and raises her middle finger, promptly leaving.

"That bitch," Godrick whispers, "You know she used to tell people that I was stalking you? And had bad photos and stuff, like what the hell?"

"Who cares, Godrick," I tell him, "Oh, can I get it in the tiny cups?"

"You want a beer shot?" the guy asks me.

"Uh, sure."

He puts the mug back under the counter and pulls out a tiny glass. He fills it up and sets it carefully in front of me. "Beer please?" he asks as the barman gives him an open bottle.

I pick up the shot glass and take a small sniff; it smells horrid, but I take a small sip anyways. It touches my tongue and I spit it out. "God, this tastes awful!" I shout.

"It's an acquired taste, honey," the barman says, "You want something sweeter?"

"So is Stockholm, and yes please."

He pours a new shot glass full of something pink, this time I taste something sharp, but still sweeter. I force all of it down and Godrick notices the disgusted look on my face.

"You're girl has fancy taste."

"Oh, that was awful!" I tell him. The barman pours another one, but this time it's clear.

"He said you want to get drunk, right? This'll do it real quick."

I sniff it and it feels like a sword being driven up my nostrils. I plug my nose and swallow it as fast as possible, but I take two gulps and cough out the second. "Oh, that burns, what is this?!" I try to say, coughing out a lung and trying to wipe up my mess.

"Vodka, honey," he tells me. The inside of my head starts to buzz around.

"Oh, this feels like cadmium—" I blurt out, stopping myself just in time.

"Like what?" they both laugh.

"Give her more of that," Godrick laughs. As he talks the world starts spinning. I try to walk away from the bar, but I trip and the stool falls over.

"Milly!" I hear Godrick's voice echo like in a long hall. I stumble about the room until I feel something like a door and fall out to the other side. The world spins faster and faster as I fall for what seems minutes until I suddenly feel a hard surface beneath me and gravel.

"Get up!" I hear a woman say. Somehow I find the strength to stand and I lean on the brick wall beside me. With a single moment of clarity I see a knife coming straight down. I raise my arm above my face and the knife cuts through the skin, but skids off the metal cords woven into my arm. I feel the vibrations reverberate throughout my entire body while under this alcoholic spell.

The blade moves again straight as an arrow towards my heart but breaks on impact of the metal in my sternum. "You bitch!" she says, and then it finally dawns on me who this is.

"Takes one to know one!" I cry back, swiftly punching her in the jaw. I feel her teeth crack apart and the whole jaw break.

"Police!" someone shouts as I drift off into blackness.

⇇ ⊙ ⇉

I wrench into the dirty, disgusting prison cell toilet, only a few feet away from Berkeley who's sitting with a mouthful of cotton and a fist-shaped break in her jawbone.

"I never would've thought I'd have you in here, Milly," he says, pausing for me to continue vomiting, "Berk, you're father paid your bail or something."

My stomach stops contracting long enough for me to breathe and looks over to see her raising her middle finger at the police officer. "I'd ask her some questions, but good lord, Milly," he laughs, "Your fathers are scheduled to come in when she stops vomiting long enough to fill out the paperwork."

My stomach contracts again, somehow ejecting more acid into the toilet bowl. I hear Berkeley incoherently mumble something, but she's probably cursing.

◁╫ ⊙ ╫▷

"Allergic to alcohol, who knew?" my father says as I continue to dry heave over the home toilet.

"You knew, didn't you—" I try to say.

He gives a long serious pause, "I did know."

I clench my fingers tighter and tighter, breaking off tiny chips of ceramic as I do. "How much—" my stomach turns, "How much—are you hiding from me?"

He pauses again, and as I stare him down a tear rolls down his face. I press against the toilet until it cracks, "How much are you hiding from me!? What are you keeping from me, Aaron!?"

"I am saving you from yourself!" he yells at me. The ceramic breaks under my hand and water starts flooding.

"Are you even my real father?" I ask, but he doesn't reply. I stumble onto my feet and walk all the way to the front door, "Spill your secrets or I'm leaving Aaron."

I nearly tumble over from my stomach contractions, but I grab onto the cabinet. I start crying and smash my hand into the metal bowl where we usually keep our keys. Through the tears, I manage to say, "Tell me, dad, or I'm going to leave."

I lift my hand, grabbing my keys from the bent around bowl. "Please, tell me," I cry, but he stands there crying too. Through the pain, I turn around and tread through the open door to the outside world.

⇇ ⊙ ⇉

The flight to Mars took four months; I had left the day when I found that Aaron had lied to me ever since I came to Earth. I didn't tell anyone I came, I just upped and left. It took about a week for me to be able to hold anything down in the space flight.

But now I'm here, in South Collestri. I may have been here for the first twelve years of life, but I was imprisoned, tortured so it's all very foreign to me; nothing to call home.

My phone starts ringing; I look down to see Godrick's face. I should've told him I left but didn't. I didn't have any personal service on the trip here, but I didn't know I'd have service on Mars.

Reluctantly, I answer the phone. "Holy shit, Milly! Where have you been?"

"Godrick, I don't want to talk right now—"

"Bullshit, Milly, I'd been worried—where are you?"

"I'm on Mars, Godrick—"

"Why the hell did you leave, like seriously, I've been calling for months and your father—" I hang up the phone, not being in the mood to talk to him. I keep walking under this reddened sky to the military base where I was quarantined after the rescue.

"There's a lone woman walking here, over." the man says at the vehicle checkpoint, "Can I help you, ma'am?"

I notice he put his finger on the trigger of his gun. "My name is Milly Haile, I want to see Fredrick."

He starts laughing and talks back into his radio, "Hey Fred, there's a girl here to see you; Milly Haile, you know her?"

The radio talks back, "Nope, what's she look like; over."

"White hair, out of your league," he says, "Ma'am I need you to stay right there, and we'll come to you—"

"I'm here to see Fredrick deWalter," I tell him.

"Oh shit," he says, placing his finger back on the gun, raising it to me. He starts walking from his post slowly; readying handcuffs for me, "Stay right where you are."

"I'm one of the fifty-four Collestri Girls—" I try to say before he cuffs me and another soldier walks me beyond the gate. A black car drives up and I'm escorted in.

"Oh my gosh! Milly!?" I hear from the other side of the car. I vaguely recognize the voice as one of the other 48.

"Mia?" I ask.

"Oh my gosh!" she squeals running over and tackling me; she feels like a brick with all the stuff she's wearing. She wiggles back and forth like a dog and squeals a bit more. "How have you been? *Where* have you been?"

"You know her?" the man asks.

"Uh, yeah! We were interned for twelve years together!" she says.

"I've been on Earth, actually; Southern Utah."

"What in the world are you doing here?"

"I actually want to see deWalter—"

"That's not a good idea; you need clearance for that." I look at the floor, thinking about what to do. "Bu-uh-t, Mr. Isaac is here today, and he might be able to work something out for you; do you remember him?"

"Could I forget?" she couldn't contain her wide smile for seeing me, this is the first time I've really had contact with any of the other girls since I left Mars. She leans over to the radio, "Take us to Mr. Isaac, over."

She looks over the other guy in here, and he's just staring at both us when Mia suddenly slaps him and he snaps back to cognition.

⊣⊢ ⊙ ⊦⊧

"He just behind this door, Milly. He hasn't had any visitors in almost a year," she says before grabbing both my shoulders and giving me a big hug again. I finally hug back and feel the probes in her back, all plugged into something. "Be careful," she emphasizes, "He's a psychopath and he'll try to get under your skin."

The door opens to my biggest fear, the most terrifying monster I know. I slowly take one step after another until he's in sight. He's strapped to a wooden chair from head to toe. He notices me and begins to creepily smile, but I march on. The moment I cross the threshold, the door closes behind me.

"Who might you be?" he asks. Anger boils within, but I try to keep my cool.

"Do you remember me, Fredrick?" I ask in return, sitting in the single steel chair.

"Hardly." he pointedly says. My face curls up in anger.

"I'm one of the surviving fifty-four girls—"

He interrupts me, "Oh, I see, would you like some coffee? Did you have trouble with the metal detector?"

"I want you to answer my questions."

"Then ask away."

"Why do all those experiments on us?"

"To build a better soldier, but as you can imagine, I was cut short —"

"Why choose us girls?"

"Women are more resilient to abuse."

I stand up from my chair and walk closer to the glass separating us. "Why are you still alive?"

He starts laughing, making me unsettled. "In the court, I needed a two thirds vote for the death penalty, and I was one vote short."

I roll up my hands into fists and drop the folder I was holding. He starts hackling at me. "Have you come to kill me yourself?"

"Don't make me."

"Your experiments succeeded in a sense, you know," he quiets down.

"How so—"

"Well, why don't you ask Mia that?" I start to tremble, but I restrain myself. "You seem to be the failure of the bunch who's visited me thus far."

"Us girls were constantly being separated, what for?"

"We wanted to see how isolation in different degrees affects each one of you. That or I just want to see what would happen if I kept you from your only friends in the world for months at a time," he starts laughing again, "I wanted to hear one blood-curdling scream at a time."

I lose control; I grab the chair and wedge it under the door handle as hard as I can. Immediately they start to bang on the door. "Milly," I hear Mia say over a speaker, "Calm down."

"I remember when Maur had her fourty-fifth bone surgery," he says. I punch the glass as hard as I possibly could, but the windows just vibrate. "We chose not to use anesthetics."

I punch the window again, and again, over and over again, screaming. I just want to kill him. The door starts pounding again and the glass finally cracks. He sounds like a hyena as he intersperses words.

"She screamed for hours as we tore her limb from limb!" The glass starts cracking more everytime I smash my hand against the glass.

"Milly, you're going to bend your knuckles!" Mia warns me, but I don't care. I'm blind to reason; I'm only out for blood. I finally notice I'm crying and wailing in grief.

"We were going to do the same to you!" he starts crying from laughter before getting serious again, "The best part is: You weren't even our favorite."

I start screaming and I feel my skin tearing apart, spraying blood all over the window as I shatter it. The door bursts open just as I punch clear through the glass. The bits spray all over deWalter; as I'm about to force my way over to strangle him, Mia gets between us and starts pushing me away. I feel her strength because I know she's using the probes to be stronger.

I thrash around trying to claw my way out, but Mia holds me down. I feel a sharp pain in my arm before I begin to blackout.

⟨⟨ ⊙ ⟩⟩

They start putting me in a five point restraint on a hospital bed as I begin to come back to consciousness. I realize where I am and I start wiggling around with whatever strength I have left. I scream when I can't budge. I scream and start crying.

"Milly, calm down," I hear Mr. Isaac's voice, "You're safe."

"I don't want to be safe!" I cry out before giving up and sobbing, "I want him dead."

"Milly, that's not for you to decide anymore," he tries to comfort me, "I—"

"Who was the Ultimo Voto!?" I scream, "tell me!"

"Milly, you don't want to know—"

"Tell me!" I sob, unable to wipe away my tears, "Who left him alive!?"

"Milly," he tries to persuade me otherwise. I thrash around in the bed, shaking it and rocking it side to side.

He sighs in defeat and whispers it to himself. "It was—" I hear with the last part inaudible.

"Say it! Say it!" I barely say as my throat begins to tighten and my nose fills with mucus. I look over to see him holding back tears.

"It was you, Milly," he says quietly, "You were chosen as the *Ultimo Voto.*"

I break. I wail and try to curl up into a ball, but restrained from doing so from the doctors treating my hand and the straps on all my limbs.

⫷ ⊙ ⫸

I was told I had been wailing and thrashing around for three entire days until I passed out from exhaustion, and for two more I was crying and refusing to eat. When I finally calmed down, they told me I put dents in my knuckles and it was inoperable; I'd be having clicks in my fingers for the rest of my life. The mesh under my skin had also been damaged and I might have nerve pains as well.

"Milly," Mia tries to comfort me beside me in the hospital bed, "Do you know why I joined the military? So I could watch him, make him fulfill his prison sentence- He's never getting out; he's going to be strapped in that chair until the day he dies."

"I let him—"

"I voted against his death too, Milly, you're not the only one."

"*I* let him live, Mia," I persist.

"twenty-eight of us voted against death; any one of us could've said yes and had him killed.

"If you want to go back to Earth, I can book you on a military ship —"

I start to cry again, "Thank you, Mia. Just, why did it have to be us?"

"The world's a dark place, Milly, there's bad people doing bad things. But you don't have to be one of them."

Tears start flowing like a raging river down my face. She leans over and hugs me tightly, "Find me on CommonPlace so we can talk, I have to go and do my job. Myrel and Misty are going to be on board with you."

"How many," I try to say, "of you?"

"Twenty-six of us joined some military, most of us here."

⊷⊙⊶

Mr. Isaac hands me a sealed, browned and reddened folder stamped 'Classified' and 'Confidential' and such. He breathes very heavily before reminding me what's inside and how I won't want to know what's in it.

"Thank you, Mr. Isaac, but it's been about time I face this," I reply.

"It's okay to forget this, live another life—"

"I know," I say, giving him a nice hug.

"Have safe travels, Milly."

⊪⊙⊫

I stare down that sealed folder; it's been weeks since I've been traveling and I have yet to open it. I'm afraid what it contains, or what to do when I finally look at it. I've been largely alone, most everyone here has a job and is doing it, but I have been visiting Myrel, Misty, and another one of their friends named Charles.

When I arrived on the ship, it took a week for me to find them. They all have their heads and hair covered, and something possessed Misty to color her hair brown over the striking white ours all are. Myrel, on the other hand, shaves her head to the skin.

As I stare, my hand stops writing whatever it is that it was writing and my mind drifts into what lies behind the waxed paper. Misty pops her head through the doorway, "Milly! All of us finally have some time off together, we're getting drinks."

"I'll come, but I don't hold my alcohol very well—"

"Then just come and get hammered, it's not like you have anywhere to be tomorrow."

I just smile and look back at the folder. "What is that anyway, sis?"

"Mr. Isaac gave me a copy of my entire file; all of it."

"Shit, really?" she asks, "I didn't know we could get those."

"I suppose you can. I—I have yet to, erm."

"Do you need to talk about anything, sis?"

"No," I tell her, "I just need to put my mind elsewhere."

⊷ ⊙ ⊶

I sit there in bed, breathing heavily from some nightmare about all our torture. It was all horrible; every time one of us didn't come back, we were always confused and depressed. Losing a sister hurt more than all the surgeries, all the experiments.

I slow my breathing, but all I can focus on is the heartbeat in my ears. I look over to that sealed folder, and for a moment I thought I saw that terrible man sitting with it in the shadow. All it was was a hanging coat. I look down at the stitches in my hand; it doesn't look the same, some of the mesh separated and I can feel the bones in my hand are different shapes now.

One step after another, I walk over to the other side of the room, finally ready to open it. My wounded hand tremors as I reach for it. Slowly I unwind the twine, fearing for my life for the first time. The overlap comes loose and I sit down on the cold metal chair.

I close my eyes and reach into the folder, feeling the thick stack of aged paper. When I open my eyes I see my first photograph from the outside world. All fifty-four of us, some of us were naked, others with tattered clothes. All of us had uneven, tangled white hair and blue eyes.

More than a couple of us had fresh surgeries and multiple scars that had yet to heal. That was the last time all fifty-four of us were together. Twelve grueling years together, only for all of us to scatter.

I set the photo aside and look at a file, initial report covering basic things, living conditions, personal accounts. The next one was a lofty medical exam with scans and doctors' notes. Next was the initial psychoanalysis: post-traumatic stress, otherwise healthy. Multiple medical follow ups and tests on my body: extreme body modification, otherwise healthy.

Therapist notes outlining every little detail we could muster. School notes over the several years we were being taught. Next, placement:

"Salvageable DNA from Forty-one, named Milly, matches a staggering nine percent DNA from Aaron Tallwalker. All background checks come clean. Possibly related within three generations.

"Forty-one, named Milly, will be placed with Aaron Tallwalker, monitored for ten years."

All it took was nine percent? Nine percent controlled my life for the past thirteen years? It went further describing mental states, learning progress reports. They were all followed by years and years of reports of my life, from Aaron. About the school, social life, etc., including an extensive report about Godrick.

I set the papers down, only being halfway through the stack and cover my mouth to keep my sobbing to a minimum. Almost everything in my new life is a lie. Thoughts about my old life, deep underground with an oppressor and fifty-four other girls and how I might want it back. I shake my head at those thoughts, reminding myself that's why those six girls couldn't escape that reality.

⫷ ⊙ ⫸

Myrel and Misty both give me big hugs before I go off in my taxi back home; I've been away for nearly six months, with nearly no correspondents with anyone. Godrick kept calling me a few times a day, but I keep rejecting them.

"Come visit us sometime, Sis!" Misty shouts out before they go out and about their military duties.

My phone starts buzzing. I look down and see Godrick's face on my screen. I clench my teeth and swipe it away to voicemail for the countless times already.

I tell my taxi to take me to a cheap hotel. As he starts driving down, I look through all the voicemails he left. Most of them are 'I'm worrying about you,' and 'I need to know when you're coming back?' A few of them are long update about what's going on. Aaron apparently is refusing contact with him too.

I notice he's driving further out of town, into the neighborhoods. "Where are you taking me?"

"I've been instructed to drive you to your caretaker's home," he replies.

"I'm 25, I don't need a caretaker, and you won't-"

"Not up to either of us, I'm just doing my job."

I start messing with the handle to open the car door, but it's locked. The rest of the drive is in silence until we arrive to my old house. I look to see Aaron pacing on the front porch. He looks over and starts running over to the car and I get out from the inside.

"Good God, Milly," he shouts running to me.

"Nine percent? Are you being serious," I tell him off, "and you think you can call me your daughter—"

He stops shy of the sidewalk, "A lot of children were taken from a lot of people Milly, you of all people should know that—"

"Nine percent?" I shout, "I—"

"Milly, don't act you know what it's like to lose a child during the war. When my wife-"

"Nine percent!" I march over and shove him back.

"Yes, nine percent!" he falls over into the grass, "My wife died during childbirth, and I never saw my child. When they told me, after twelve frickin' years they tell me they've found what could be my daughter—"

"Nine—nine damn percent?" I start crying my eyes out.

"Who really knows who your father is? I know that you are the only person I'm related to that's still alive," he starts to cry too; "I didn't pass an opportunity like that, to possibly have my daughter back."

I slowly fall over, leaning onto the white picket fence, crying. He crawls over to hug me, to mourn with me. Something inside me hugs him back and we sit there for who knows how long, crying together.

⊶ ⊙ ⊷

After we both went back inside, I toss my bag aside and start drinking tea that he had made me. A hard knock at the door startles me Aaron goes to see who it is when it knocks again. He opens the door, and Godrick is there.

"Is Milly—"

"Now's not a good time, Godrick—"

"Holy shit, Milly!" he shouts, pushing through my dad and rushing over to me, "What the hell?"

"Godrick, you don't under—"

"I don't understand what?!" he yells, "You just ghost me for months and I find out you're on Mars—"

"Shut up, Godrick!" I yell back, standing off at him, "I needed to sort out some problems—"

"No shit, Milly! We work them out *together!*"

"I needed to do it alone—"

"No!" he shouts, raising up both his arms, "Me, and you, Milly, that means we do it together!"

"Get out Godrick!"

"No! I said I would be by your side and here I am."

"Get out!" I start pushing him away, but he wraps his arms around and pulls me close.

"Please, let me help," he tenderly whispers, but I still push him away.

"Godrick, I need to do this alone," I whisper through my own tears, "Please go."

"No—" he says before I push him off me and run to my bedroom. I overhear Aaron escort him out of the house, but it's not soon before my tears drown that out too. My room has gotten dusty, it's the exact same as I left it months ago.

I don't want it to be this way, it shouldn't have to be this way, but it is. It shouldn't have been me, or Aaron or Godrick, but it is. Life should be fair, but it isn't. I don't want to have to fix all these problems and move on.

Today's the day I became an adult, and not a scared child whose been sliced open countless times and mutilated and tortured, whose been trapped for twelve years with only a dictator and an insane surgeon.

It shouldn't be this way, but it is.

Magic in the New Age

◖◉◗

LIKE CLOCKWORK, the horn blows into the English fog as I hang from some rope overhanging the ocean water. The salty air stings my dry lips as the wind blows, but we're almost to shore.

Months at sea on a steamboat don't do the body well. "Sir! We're not going to rescue you if you fall into the water again!" a crewman shouts up to me.

"I'm enjoying myself!" I shout back.

"Suit yourself!"

I jump down to the deck and take a deep breath of the British air. Uncle was right, this is going to be good for me; I can feel it, despite how much it's costing him.

"Land ho!" a seaman calls. I look out, but see nothing but fog and a faint glow of a lighthouse. That is my cue to go to my keep and ensure my possessions are still mine to take to shore.

The inside of the boat is damp and humid enough to swim through, but my door is still locked. I find my room exactly as I left it. Quickly, I start to fold my clothing and store them in my chest ready to leave as soon as we dock to shore.

An attendant comes down the hall ringing a bell. "Ready to dock! Be ready to dock!" he shouts as he walks passed all the keeps.

I grab the two handles on the clothing chest and heave to lift it. Solid hardwood, as luxurious as it is, weighs as much as stone. Slowly, I lift it inch by inch until it's over my other chest, the one on wheels. The ship begins to jostle around as we make for shore.

"Be orderly! One at a time, you'll all get off!" one of the seamen yells, ringing a bell as the hoard of passengers make their way to dry land.

A large, fat man starts to shove into my belongings, trying to push me along. "You got a problem?" I ask, propping my foot under the wheels to keep my luggage still.

"Just the one in front of me, mate."

"If you want to push past me, you're going to have to try harder."

He tries to push me along to close the gap between me and the several people moving ahead of me, but I hold my ground and don't let my things move.

"Ye bastard, just get to shore!" he shouts at me. I let go of my things and start pulling them along. I take a deep breath of this British air and get ready for my work here.

◄◄ ⊙ ►►

"Bring these up to my room please," I tell the busboy.

"Sir, in all due respect," he says, "They're too heavy for me to carry."

I sigh and put my watch away. "Then I'll help you."

I take one side and he takes the other and we heave the first chest into the air. Step by step we make it up the stairs to the first bend.

"Um, sire," the boy says, "It, uh, won't fit."

"Are you sure?" I ask.

I see him look around and pull the chest, wedging it further between the walls. "Um, I'm sure."

I whisper some spells under my breath, causing the chest to become flexible.

"I'm going to push on three, boy!" I shout.

"Heave!" we say in unison, and the chest moves through the corner. The walls and chest creak and moan as the wood bends like rubber.

"Oh, gee," the kid says, "I didn't think that would fit." Step by step, we make our way up the stairs to my room in the inn. We get to the room, my first time seeing it, and set the chest by the foot of my bed.

"Little small, but it's alright," I tell him, "Help me with the next one?" I look over to see him taking a deep breath and rubbing his arms.

⊪ ⊙ ⊪

My dear nephew: I've arranged for you to attend a ball this coming Wednesday evening. You will go and enjoy the party. You will find Sir Abram, offer my letter of introduction, and study under him for the duration of your trip.

I fold the letter from my dear uncle and set it aside. "What are you thinking, Uncle?" I ask myself, "What am I going to do with you?"

⊪ ⊙ ⊪

The orchestra plays a solemn, melancholy song; slow, but in perfect pitch. All those who are dancing sway along with the slow beat, but many are sticking around the edges of the room to converse with one another.

A young lady walks up to me. "Dirty clothes, not even fancy enough to come, yet here you are," she criticizes me.

"I work in the clothes I wear," I reply, "I don't have anything better than what I'm wearing."

I scan this young woman in her big dress, corset too tight; beautiful really, with painted white skin, but her hair is a beautiful brown. "How may I help you, young lady?"

"I notice things when they're out of place," she tells me, "And you're like a nail in a floorboard, darling."

"I suppose I am," I say, "You seem to fit quite well."

She walks up close to me and rests her hand on my vest, brushing the wrinkles out of it. "What do you say we escape this dreary party?"

I run my finger through the bottom part of a lock of hair. "I'm afraid I have too much respect for women, you see."

"I think you're guessing wrong," she says, "I want to go somewhere where I'll have a better time—"

"Such as?" I ask.

"Perhaps a restaurant," she replies, biting her rosy red lips, "Eat some pastries, perhaps?"

"I'm looking for Sir Abram, do you know him?"

She chuckles, grabbing a small treat from a nearby tray. "Why, of course!" she tells me, "He's my father."

◀▌⊙▐▶

She leads me to a back room, where it's ice cold. She takes me into a study, where I see an older man drawing on old parchment.

"Yes, my dear?" he greets the young lady.

"He was looking for you, father," she replies.

"I have a letter of introduction from my Uncle, Sir Abram," I add in.

"No one has called me 'Sir Abram' in many years, boy." I hand him the letter from my uncle, where he takes one look at it and sets it aside. "Why has your uncle sent you here?"

"To study under you, sir?" I tell him, "It's all in the letter, though I'm not sure what—"

"I do not take apprentices, boy, not after your uncle stole one of my books."

"Over a book?" I ask, "Either way, I must insist."

"Oh, would you father?" the girl pleads. The man takes in a deep breath and sighs.

"Anything for you, daughter," he says, "If you can tell me what spell was Hamilton most famous for?"

"I'm afraid I don't understand," I tell him, "Hamilton was a politician." I look down at what he was drawing: geometric patterns over circles; incredibly intricate and complex.

"Do you understand these patterns?" he asks me.

"I don't sir," I explain, "The ones at home don't look quite like that."

"At home?" he asks.

"My Uncle and I are pig and cotton farmers. We use circular patterns in the fields to bring rain in the dry seasons."

"Is that what the great magician has been up to?" he says to himself, "Farming?"

"It's honest work," I say, "So you will apprentice me?"

"Oh please, father," the girl pleads him, holding her hands together.

◄◄ ⊙ ►►

"Tell me, boy," Mr. Abram begins, "How proficient are you in the magical arts?"

"Magic?" I ask, "I beg your pardon?"

"Yes, Arthor. If you don't know, then we'll have to start on history first." Mr. Abram begins searching his library, looking through the exquisite collection of books. "Ilus Everaurd was the most prominent magician—"

"Sorry, I beg your pardon," I say, "I just didn't think there were any magicians other than my uncle sir and myself."

"You think you're the only magician in the entire world?" he chastises me, "Who do you think taught your Uncle?"

"My uncle doesn't talk much about those things." I sit down on a stool in the middle of the room, overlooking some circles. "But Ilus Everaurd, I have heard of him."

"What do you know about him?" he asks.

I think about it for a moment. "I suppose I don't know much, his name has only came up briefly."

"He's the greatest magician of his time!" he shouts, pulling out a book from his collection and handing it to me. "Read this over, it'll bring you up to speed on his accomplishments."

"Now, sir?" I ask.

"Yes!" he turns back around to look through the other books. I open the book to its first page, with circles drawn as part of the title page. I ready to touch it, but something seems to be pulling my hand away from it. "Protection spell for the longevity of the book, my boy. Pay no mind to it."

"Yes sir." I flip the page and see some illustrations of what Ilus had used as educational spells in his day. His early life as a refugee in the British conquest of mainland Europe by the king. It goes on and on, but rarely mentions his magical achievements, only personal details about his early life.

The next chapter seemingly talks about the Black Hands, Ilus' involvement and how they overthrew the king and conquered the Nords. After a 'Great Battle', Ilus killed the leader of the Black Hands and disbanded them.

"Sir, this book has no magic, it's just—"

"A history book," he interrupts, "Since you have newly heard of Ilus Everaurd."

"Sir, but I'd like to know the magic he used."

"It's another book."

"Ah, yes, I suppose." I flip through the pages, sparsely containing the old spells as a demonstration. I find one that's particularly interesting, transferring heat from one spot to another. I set my hand on the spells and close my eyes to focus.

"It won't work, boy," Mr. Abram tells me, "Spells that old don't work anymore."

"Why not?" I ask.

"Magic changes over time, it's not the same as it used to be."

"I suppose I'll be here a while, if I'm reading history books all day," I say jokingly.

"I have all day," he replies.

◀◦▶

"This bread is lovely!" Sir Abram's daughter exclaims with a squeal. I've taken Holly to the market while Sir Abram goes out to do his work, casting spells for the wealthy, I presume.

"It's bread, Holly," I say, thanking the baker, "You shouldn't break it until you're ready to eat the entire thing or it'll get stale."

"My father will just give you more money for more bread." She grabs my arm and we move further along the market on this street. She grabs random fruit from the stands and continues to devour it as I hand the person the money.

"You'll get fat if you keep eating this much," I tell her.

"I haven't eaten since noon yesterday for this exact reason," she retorts, "So what are you working on with my father?"

"He specifically requested that I not tell you." We finally find a spot to enjoy some of the half-eaten fruit away from the bustle of the street.

"Why?" she persists, "Is he a secret wizard or something? I read a book based on that exact story, once upon a time."

"He's keeping me in his library most of the time, reading history books, though," I tell her, "Boring as all, that is."

I tear some bread and stuff my mouth with it, enjoying the taste of it on my tongue. The British air is not as good as back home in Virginia. "You shouldn't keep your secrets, Arthor." she says, "You'll die one day without letting them out in the world."

❮❮ ⊙ ❯❯

I look through this book, with actual spells I can use this time. Sir Abram has me copying down spells as practice. I sit there copying one down on a piece of parchment, carefully tracing out the lines with some ink.

"And this one, what does it do?" I ask.

"It magnifies the magnetic field of an object, making it act like a false compass," he explains, pointing to certain embedded patterns.

"I see." I finish off the circle. I place my hand over it along with a piece of iron. I focus deeply on the spell, but it refuses to be cast.

"Modern magicians require foci to cast spells, one you don't have. One Sir Herman once said a hundred years that our earthly bodies are unable to focus the natural magic because we are imperfect."

"Doesn't seem right," I say. I think the special item Uncle told me I was to present to a group of magicians, how it will 'Focus My Study'.

"There's no other explanation, he was a great magician himself." I go about tracing out another one of these as practice and command, unable to cast them myself.

"Tomorrow, Arthor, I meet with a council of local magicians, I shall present you to them."

"Council?" I ask.

"Yes, the ten greatest magicians of the county meet together to discuss, well, *magical* matters,"

◀◀ ⊙ ▶▶

I look at the council: seven old gentlemen, two overdressed women like they're getting portraits, and Sir Abram. "Oh, how lovely, new blood!" one the woman says; Lady Estreech, I believe.

"Good evening everyone," Sir Abram announces, "I've taken on an apprentice, and he will provide a demonstration for you."

I reach into my pocket and feel the focus that Sir Abram loaned me. Something isn't right about these people, and I don't want to play into their games. I did bring my own focus: a wand from my Uncle's private collection of magical items.

I leave Sir Abram's focus in my pocket and pull out the wand from my sleeve. Slowly they all become wide-eyed, especially Lady Estreech. I point the wand at the table, where Sir Abram prepared a spell for me.

I whisper my own spell underneath my breath and the paper begins to brown, and then blacken, while a small flame begins to take shape into a stallion and dance around on the table.

"Oh, my!" Lady Estreech exclaims, "I haven't seen one of those in ages! Where did you get that? I must have it."

"I'm sorry, Lady Estreech, it belongs to my Uncle and is not for sale," I tell her.

"Quite the recital, Arthor," Sir Abram says, clearly angry or upset at something.

⊶⊙⊷

I hear them debating, or plainly arguing, behind the closed door. "So, erm... How did your first impressions go?" Holly asks me.

"Controversial," I reply.

She chuckles, "What did you do in there, which turned so many heads?"

"Again, you're father has requested that I keep that from you, Holly."

She leans over to lay her hand on mine. "It'll be alright, don't worry."

"Holly, my dear," I begin.

"Yes, Arthor?" she answers.

"It's been about half a year since I arrived here in England," I pause to collect my thoughts.

"Yes?" She persists.

I hear an outburst from beyond the door, *I need that wand!* I hear from Lady Estreech. Followed by, *We all want it!* From someone else.

"Come back with me," I confess.

"Where?" she laughs.

"To Virginia; to America," I finish. She starts laughing hysterically, but slowly dies down.

"Really?" she asks.

"Yes, really." She grabs my hands and leans over.

"My father would hate me for it," she continues to laugh a little.

⧏ ⊙ ⧐

"I was hoping you'd be interested in our magical artifact collection, Arthor," Lady Estreech tells me, walking me down a musty hallway. She opens a door, and as I peek through, I'm amazed at what's inside.

There are skulls with inscriptions, weapons with spells etched so carefully on the surface. There are so many pieces of jewelry as well. "This sword belonged to the great Ilus Everaurd, you know," She points to a mysterious weapon made of small, sharp links; each one carefully inscribed in its own set of spells. "I'm only missing twenty-three more pieces, including the scabbard; I hope to finish it by my fortieth birthday," she exclaims.

She also shows me a spear with a large metal circle towards the tip, carved with spells as well. "It was common for the era to carve the spells into your weapon, I'm sure you're wondering."

"These are quite magnificent specimens, Lady Estreech," I reply to all her rambling, "My Uncle has a collection of his own back in Virginia; though not as big."

"What does he have and is willing to sell?"

"I'm afraid I don't know what's inside, I've only had glimpses of what he has," I reply, "I don't think he's wanting to sell either."

"What a shame," she says.

I see a ring with a large, smooth metal bead instead of a jewel. The ring itself is a dull gold, full of scratches, but the metal bead is still perfectly smooth. "I see that's caught your eye, it's a focus ring: the jewel is a wolfram bead," she explains, "That one may or may not have belonged to said Sir Everaurd."

◀▌ ⦿ ▐▶

"Arthor," Sir Abram begins to speak, "I believe, you are more talented than you let me on to believe."

"Yes, Sir Abram, I am."

"Show me, if you would," he commands.

I pull out Uncle's wand and cast a particular spell I've been creating. Illuminated strings, hundreds of them, fly out from the tip of the wand and latch themselves onto any surface.

"Incredible, Arthor," he says, "What can it do though, it's useless without a purpose."

"I'd rather not pull all the books off the self," I reply, releasing the spell, "Theoretically it can be used to pull any object, collapsing a cavern even."

"You say this as you know," he persists on my words, "I've been hearing a rumor that you're going back to America."

"Yes, Sir Abram," I tell him, "I'm afraid I've learned all I will here."

"With my daughter, I've been told," he asserts, "I forbid it!"

"All due respect, I don't think you have a choice."

"Begone, Arthor!" he shouts.

I stand from my stool and close my folder containing all the spells I've been working on and being on my way out. Holly looks at me as I make my way out, latching onto my arm as we make our way to my inn to pack my things.

"Give me your hand, Holly," I ask.

"Why so forward, sir?" she jokes.

"Just give me your hand," I say, taking her hand and sliding on that ring from Lady Estreech's collection.

"I would at least expect a jewel, Arthor."

The boat hits a wave and jostles around a little. "Trust me, this is much more valuable than any jewel," I reply.

"I'll trust you then," she says, tightening her hold on my arm through the British fog.

The Mazzatello Traipse

◄◄◎►►

Herded like cattle, tens of thousands of people. Another train comes rolling in. It's massive, able to fit hundreds of us in each car. They're colored copper-green and modeled after local traditional architecture.

Many of us are pushed onto the car, people of all walks of life. When the train begins marching on, I find myself next to one of the natives on this same journey. She smiles and greets me in her language. I'm learned in this language, so I greet her back. She smiles once again and asks for my name.

"You'll never be remembered here with a name like that," She says, "I will remember you as a friend."

It wasn't long until the train's destination was in sight; a great white wall, marked 'Death' in their native language. Dark red streaks flow down from the hundreds of notches along the top of the wall like tears from the heavens. I recollect and realize the young miss has disappeared into the crowd.

The train travels closer, revealing the hoard of corpses at the base of the great white wall. The train passes through the wall, revealing the inner city, but that's not our destination. The train stops, and we're lead away in single-file lines, up the steps to the top of the wall. Thousands of people are here before us.

We climb the steps, higher and higher, surrounded by more strangers. The ones I knew are gone, separated from me earlier. We march up the wall, all the way to the top, where our destination lies.

As the bevy travels ever closer, fate becomes apparent; I look ahead and observe:

"Last words?" the soldiers repeat time and time again. The responses range from prayers to curses, but destiny arrives all the same.

"Last words?" a soldier says.

The man prays as he is forced down onto the wall. A wedge is placed above him, pressing on his skull and another soldier stands above. A beetle is swung, crashing down the wedge, killing the man. Without any care, the stiff is thrown over the wall to be forgotten by the soldiers and to show the world.

I fear the young miss is meeting the same fate as the rest of us, even as I await mine. Another man is forced down and murdered. This time he stands up with his skull crushed in, but with enough stamina to curse them. A soldier shoots him through his battered head and disposes of the corpse over the wall.

I look at the high ranked soldier, begging, "Please." But with the glare that welcomed my plea, it became apparent that he wasn't doing this because of instruction or coercion, but because it was the true desire of his blackened, evil heart. For you can not stop a man from his true desires.

Obadiah's Legend

⊩◎⊪

THIS IS A TALE from long ago, as told by my people, passed down from generation to generation, and now I am here to recount it to you. It is one of the many legends of the desert. Are you ready?

Yes, I am ready.

It started in one of the earliest settlements of the desert…

⊩⊙⊪

"Help! Help!" I hear a man yell through the streets, "I need the help of Obadiah!"

I rub the bridge of my nose at the sound of another man crying for help. I carried supplies when the asses became too tired trekking through the desert. I led the people through the night by the stars and commanded the sandstorms as a child. Even still, I am the one they call for all their needs, from tossing the bales to digging deeper wells; it's all medial work for a normal man, not for me.

"It is I, Obadiah!" I call out to the man rushing through the crowded streets.

"There is a wall approaching! It cannot be stopped!" he tells me.

"A wall of what?" I inquire.

"Stone, it's a moving wall," he explains, "Me and my men were surveying the land and a wall began to approach."

"Show me."

"It's a double league out to the west."

I rub the bridge of my nose once again. "It's a double league out? And you come to me in a panic?"

"It cannot be stopped by anything but you, and it will be on the horizon in two days' time."

I let out a disappointed sigh, and begin my walk to the western edge of the settlement. "Where are you going?" the man asks.

"You said it is to the west and will be here in two days' time, so I will go and stop this wall of stone. Come, follow me."

We begin walking and he becomes frantic. "Are you not going to take a mule with you?" he asks in his mania.

"I need no mule," I tell him, "We've come to the edge of the city, which way is this unstoppable wall?"

He points towards the setting sun and says, "It's a double league in that direction."

"Tai!" I shout, summoning my power. My legs leap and launch me into the air, leaving behind a sand cloud from whence I stood. The wind rushes around my body as I soar through the air.

Not a moment's whit later and I crush the ground under my immense strength. The sand settles down back to the earth, and I see this unstoppable wall of stone the man spoke of, inching forward.

"No stone wall is unstoppable to me," I whisper to myself.

I fill my lungs with air, giving strength to my arms, and I shout, "Dao!" My fist lands a blow to the wall and it cracks under the force; portions fall away, dust crawls into the air, and the wall ceases its movement.

I hear a heartbeat surge in fear. "Dao!" I shout once more to give strength to my punch, and I thrust my fingers through this unstoppable stone wall, breaking it's protective barrier. The heart beats faster as my fingers find their way around it.

I grasp a man behind the wall and tear him from his place before me. "You are pathetic," I tell him, tossing him to the ground.

"You know nothing of the arts," I chastise the man.

"Momr!" the man shouts as he casts a bolt of lightning at me.

The bolt travels slowly to my eyes; it's weak in power, and I deflect it with a simple slap of my hand.

"You are nothing," I tell him.

That was so long ago…

❮❯ ⊙ ❮❯

"Momr!" he shouts, casting lightning from his hands. It strikes close to my heart. I let a whisper of pain escape my lips as I recoil my fists to land a single blow against him.

His speed is beyond mine, but he lacks in strength and skill, thus he uses powerful but unpredictable techniques. My attack swiftly flies beside his head, but he is now within the range of my kicks.

My leg raises, and I enchant the muscles to thrust with the strength of a storm into his body. The force sends him into the ground, spraying sand everywhere. He coughs blood into the soil as he recoups.

"You disgust me!" he cries out, "Every time we fight each other, you show me mercy!"

"You're not worthy to die in battle," I gently replies.

"Momr!" he thrusts his lightning at me. It is still weak and slow so I step to the side to allow it to pass.

"You endanger my people, you disgrace the arts. If you come again to perform anything other than repentance for your transgressions, it will be our last encounter."

I spit at his feet and launch myself away back to the settlement.

◀◀ ⊙ ▶▶

"Obadiah," A man shouts to me while I plow the land. This land has turned very fertile since we relocated all that time ago.

"Mind the crops," I whisper to myself.

He runs to me through the grains, arriving out of breath. "There's a soldier from the Empire here, he calls for all masters of the arts."

I drop the plow, and stretch my back, "I'm no master; I was expelled from the monasteries."

The man soaks his hand in the soil and rubs it on his head to stay cool under the sun. "The King has called for you by name."

"And what ultimatum has he brought me?"

"The King's army will come to invade."

"Very well," I relay my message, "Let them come, for I will not bow to the King."

Time went on, but they did not come for many days. Not even the King's army could come this far into the desert. We're not near the coasts or fertile land; no oasis for many leagues.

"The King will respect your rejection of the summons, but the king will enforce a tax; not of gold, but of your food.

"You've made this land very fertile and we happen to be in a famine."

"I will not bow to any king."

The King did send a troop and two masters to collect this tax; the people freely gave to appease the King. But they came and demanded more in each return. Another master was sent to enforce the tax, but the people bowed and swore peace.

"Obadiah!" A woman shouts at me, "They will come, and they will destroy everything we've worked for!"

"If they come, they will not find us. If they find us, not a single soul will make it back."

"How could you possibly know that?"

How could he?

"Shi Dai Bu!" my soul bellows to the earth. Turbulence circles the city, blowing sand all around..

The troops did return, only to find the desert with not even an oasis for several leagues.

⫷ ⊙ ⫸

There is an elderly man walking through the settlement, but unable to see the people or the asses, not even a brick. "What a curious place, here," he speaks, seemingly to the illusion.

"This is quite a powerful illusion someone has cast here, I cannot see a single thing but the expanse of the desert," he continues speaking, "I've come seeking the Master who made an entire settlement vanish, never to be seen again."

"'Tis I, Obadiah," I announce. The elderly man opens one of his squinted eyes.

"My name is Abd al Hakim, a Servant of the Wise. I've come to impart some wisdom to you, Obadiah."

"Make it so, and part from here."

Abd al Hakim reaches out, and touches my very soul; *The King craves your defeat and will stop at nothing to see your corpse.*

He parted and we had peace for twenty years. The King's armies did come searching, but never found what they longed to find. Many of the troops were lost to the dunes. During this time, they desecrated the desert that gave us protection and life. Masters had turned entire dunes to stone and ripped holes in the earth searching for me.

⊹⊙⊹

"I will go and search for the King," I announce to the people.

"The desert will consume you," a man replies.

"The desert will let me pass, and bow to my will."

"The King will unleash his entire army for you."

"The King will bow to my will, and I will not die."

He set out searching for the King, but the King did not reside in the city from whence we came. He did not reside in the palaces built for Kings from the past. Obadiah searched for ten years and did not find him.

The desert aided him, guided Obadiah to an oasis to give strength to his aged body so he could continue to search once more and end this King's reign. Five years passed, and Obadiah returned to his city, which expanded its reach into the desert, and became very prosperous. The Hidden Village remained a safe place for all who sought its refuge.

Abd al Hakim appears in the mirage of the scorching heat and glass beneath my feet. He says, "Your journey is not complete, o' Obadiah, the King still awaits you. Go and travel more, and you will find him on the second thousandth day hence. You *will* find him."

He searched for another five years, and on the second thousandth day from talking with Abd al Hakim, Obadiah found a palace that was erected where an ancient monastery once stood.

"I seek the King of this land," I speak to the guardian of the gate.

"Very well, but I require payment for you to enter, for lifting this gate is strenuous."

"Then I will lift it."

"This gate weighs thirty loads; an old man cannot lift it."

I approach the gate, and my soul chants it's spells to give me strength; I lift the gate and enter into the palace.

"Who goes there? I am the King and I will allow no stranger in my presence."

"It is I, Obadiah."

The man turns around to face me, and there he stands before me, cloaked in fine linens and silk.

"Now you wouldn't hurt a frail old man, now would you, Obadiah?" he asks.

"I told you the next time we meet; I would not show you mercy. This ends here."

"Momr Kai!" A streak of lightning is cast at me, and it is overpowering. The ground breaks beneath me and my clothes burn and become shredded.

I utter my needs of strength to the desert all around, and the desert calls back to me. I receive my strength, and I jump to the King and strike him on his head. He rebounds and backs to the wall behind him.

"You are still a coward," I tell him.

He wipes away the blood draining from his mouth. "I'm no weakling."

"Kai!" he shouts, and a concussive wind swirls about, and the wall of the palace breaks down. With his summoned strength, he slings a large stone at me and the palace crumbles.

The weakened material shatters and turns to dust in front of my fist. "Fight me!" I shout, launching myself to him.

❮❮ ⊙ ❯❯

He summons his lightning to suspend him in the air and thrusts a powerful bolt at me. I attempt to redirect it by catching the bolt with my fingers, but it slips ever so between my fingers, striking my body.

It's enough force to knock me down to the desert below, now scattered with the crumbling pieces of the palace. Sand begins to surround me as I'm continually knocked into the ground by lightning raining down from above as if it were a storm from the gods.

The flashing lights slow until I can see his fist coming down to strike me. My reflexes are faster than his speed, and I swiftly push his hand into the bedrock beside me. I drive him into the stone, and flee the crater.

Another bolt of lightning streaks out of the crater and misses me by mere cubits. An explosion of light and dust sends a shockwave that carries me to the ground.

"Don't think you can get away from me this easily, Obadiah," I hear behind me, followed by lightning to my back.

How did he get there so quickly?

I fall to the ground in agony, and I try to recoup my strength, using my incantations to no avail.

"I'll show you mercy by letting you see your precious paradise burn."

I bite my tongue, and let the blood drip into the desert. "You'll never find it."

He thrusts his foot into my side. "Then I'll have to take it from you.

"Ara Shayana!"

The world begins to shake, the sky as blood, the very sand becoming as solid stone and the very image of him transforms into a toad with a curled tongue.

"No!" I cry, "Shi Kai!"

Two of my fingers move through this powerful illusion and slice through the grotesque toad. This illusion is gone, but so is the barrier of the hidden village.

This boy falls to the ground with a gouge across his face.

"Damn you, Obadiah. But at least I found it." he reaches down into the ground, and pulls out a serpent. "Kai!"

The spell cracks the very bedrock beneath all, and it begins to collapse into a sinkhole. I pray to the gods to keep my descent into the earth beneath gentle.

"This ends Obadiah," He announces to the empty catacombs, "I will kill him!"

He turns to me, and we both ready for the final blow. The tension grows and I watch very closely at his small movements.

The spirit of Abd al Hakim guides me, readying me for this final moment, perhaps of my death.

"Momr Kai!" he cries mightily and his voice shakes the catacombs. The light overcomes my sight, but Abd al Hakim guides my fingers to catch the lightning.

The energy of 10,000 days of sun is imbued in my very being, even my soul. Abd al Hakim departs, and my vision returns to see the soon to collapse cave. There he was, defeated, unable to regain strength.

"So this is the end," he tells me, "Goodbye, old friend."

I release the power tenfold upon him. This was the end for both of us. I feel the power eat away at both of our bodies until... nothing.

Thus ends the Legend of Obadiah.

Incredible.

The Path I Walk

I HAVE a single question: Why did I have to suffer so much? I follow Him, but I stop in my tracks. He asks why I've stopped. I reply that I have a question.

"And what do you desire to know?" He asks me.

"Why was life pain? Why was *my* life pain?" I give my conjecture, "My life was filled with heartbreak and agony, my body failed me and so did the people around me through their greed and selfishness."

"Have ye faith?"

"Yea Lord, I do."

"Then walk the path I walk," He tells me, as we begin on our journey once more, "Do you know all things?"

"No, I do not," I tell Him, "But there was little in my life I knew save that it was pain and heartbreak. I lived alone and I died alone."

"I suffered by your side so that I might understand."

"But why can't *I* understand?"

"You know not all things, but you have an eternity to learn and progress."

"Why an eternity?"

"The journey of a thousand miles starts with a single step, one after another.

"You may run, or walk the journey, but it is one step nonetheless."

People Before Pride

◄◄ ◎ ►►

THE CLOCK ticks noon, and we begin my audience with our country's leader. "Let us commence," the president commands.

"Good afternoon, Mr. President," I greet him, "I've compiled the available information on population growth I could find for the past century.

"The growth is out of control, six and a half billion people in mainland alone, it's going to collapse our infrastructure eventually, not to mention the excessive spread of STI conditions; we have to institute federal regulations on reproduction—"

"Objection!" another one of the female presenters shouts, "We founded this country on personal freedom. We're one of the last countries in the world to stay that way. Imagine the mass opposition to such regulations."

I begin again, "Most of Asia has instituted strict and controlled human reproduction with great success. Steady population decrease with acceptable levels of genetic diversity, even by our standards."

She starts her objection once more, "I've read his proposition. He means to *force* every capable citizen into heterosexual relations and force a federal and scientific board controlled reproduction and adoption program. This simply violates the personal freedoms we've fought so hard to enjoy in this country."

I continue my presentation, "I'm proposing that all citizens be restricted single child reproduction with willing participants approved by a medical board. This allows for the personal choice to have children, but keeps a steady population decrease and standard genetic diversity."

"And what about those in homosexual relationships?" the president asks me.

"As I've described in my written proposition, allowing the considerable size of the homosexual population to squander their contribution to genetic diversity would make the desired population decrease nearly impossible to achieve. Forty-three percent of our country's population lives in homosexual marriages, this simply bottlenecks genetic diversity. Allowing this will utterly destroy the diversity in DNA for our citizens on any account."

"They could just be left as they are, and it is *still* possible to achieve standard genetic diversity and population decrease and *still* have their personal freedoms intact. I had this independently verified."

"Madam," the president says, "You're in a same-sex marriage, correct?"

"Yes, Mr. President."

"And sir, you're unmarried, yes?"

I pause for a second, pondering how much they know about me, "Yes, sir. I'm unmarried."

"By choice or incident?" he asks me.

"Undetermined," I reply honestly.

"Let's bring this presentation to a recess, shall we? My stomach isn't sitting well. Let's rejoin in an hour."

◂◂ ⊙ ▸▸

I rub my face with warm water, looking in the mirror, questioning once again, this whole debacle. "You're persistent on this, aren't you?" the woman presenter asks me, standing beside me in the mirror.

"I choose to be, yes," I reply.

"Do you know why I'm opposed to this?"

"My proposal doesn't exactly work in your favor, so I can make an educated guess."

"Your proposal would be forcing me *and* my wife to have children with men we wouldn't even know. And you'd be forcing us to give our children away to other families."

"Not exactly," I say, "I understand-"

She leans into my ear, "You understand nothing. We all know your secret and why you aren't married. This'll hurt you too."

I stand straight and look at her sternly, "As a representative of this country's people, it is my sworn duty to keep the people's best interests at the forefront of my legislation. Unlike you, I put the people's well being before my own."

"The primary interest of the government and the people who run it is the protection of the interests and freedoms of the people."

"Well, when you have to legislate over nearly seven billion people in your borders, you make tough choices."

"I apologize for the frequent recesses, I've had food poisoning these past few days, but let us resume."

She and I lock in a distasteful gaze. "I believe my proposal in its early draft can lay a good groundwork to ensure the survival and well being of the human race, if not now, then for generations to come."

"Any final rebuttal for you, Madam?" he asks.

"Freedom of the person before the needs of the people, sir. That's my rebuttal."

"I see, and for you? Any last words?" he asks me.

"Humanity comes before personal desires."

Sam, The Unsung

❮❰ ◎ ❱❯

LOOKING BACK at my life's journey, it's a relatively short one, especially compared to Rythlen's. At the time of writing, I am twenty-four years of age. My journey started at my birth, like many others. The Elders of the church used to vaguely tell me of my origin. A woman was passing through town with a child. When the woman finally found one of the Elders, she offered the child as a sacrifice to Selune, the Goddess of the Moon. Though this isn't an actual practice of this church, she abandoned the child in the care of the Elders in the midst of the night.

I grew up in this church, a separate stem of the church of Selune; a church I wasn't fond of at the time, nor one I wanted to follow. My early years were spent in education, grooming me to be an Elder. I had even learned the Infernal and Celestial languages as part of my education. They had me recite scripture after scripture nearly every day. Though, by age twelve, I had made it very clear to the Elders that it wasn't my desire to become a priest, missionary, or an Elder later in my life.

⇇ ⊙ ⇉

Elder Dorian and I walk into the courtyard, towards one of the corners away from the others walking about the area.

"You wished to meet with me."

"I don't want to be one of you."

"And why not? It's a privilege to be chosen to be an Elder—"

"I don't want to be an Elder."

"But you've been given such an opportunity."

"It's not the life I want to live. I wish to travel to faraway places."

"You could be a missionary?" Elder Dorian persists.

"No, I don't want to be a missionary," I insist.

Turning, I glance toward the open area of the courtyard. Elder Dorian follows my eyes, landing on two students of a different school of study, sparing with each other. Back and forth they move, swinging fallen tree branches like swords.

"I see," Elder Dorian says, understanding, "Perhaps we should switch your field of study then."

❮❮ ⊙ ❯❯

Back in those days, I had dreamed of traveling to far off places to meet creatures beyond my, then current, imagination. I had heard of Elves, who paved their cities in gold and fine craftsmanship. Stories circulated about how Dwarves burrowed into the ground and created elaborate cities and tunnels deep under the earth. I greatly desired to see these things for myself.

But, despite my yearnings, the Elder wanted to keep me close, and offer me guidance in my life as a way to fill the void of parenthood. They changed my study to combat training and other survival skills. I was charged to protect the temple and HighTower from an impending threat. Rumors told of a dark army, comprised of grotesque monsters and sorcerers, coming from the east and destroying city after city, were becoming common from the travelers passing the temple.

These travelers told of rival factions of varied species coming together to fight this approaching army. Personally, I wasn't too worried. After all, the threat was so far away from us.

❮❮ ⊙ ❯❯

I overhear some of the older guards talking with a traveler at the gate.

"It's true, I saw a clan of Orcs marching alongside Dwarves, heading east toward the front lines," the traveler tells them.

"I find that hard to believe, but you're welcome to resupply here at HighTower."

I stop listening and continue to slouch in my seat, allowing my spear to lean on me between my shoulder and neck.

◂◂ ⊙ ▸▸

It was three or four years since I heard those rumors as a temple guard. As time passed, increasing numbers travelers came with even more outlandish stories, speaking of creatures I'd never heard of in my human home of HighTower. They told how the armies of darkness were pushing back every force that opposed them, inching closer and closer to our home. The Elders took notice of these rumors; the people were concerned for their safety.

The Elders urged the people to remain calm, and that the war was going to be over well before it came near HighTower. They used parables, analogical stories, along with plenty of scripture to help the people remain calm.

They talk about how the land would go through times of light and darkness, just as the moon and the Goddess Selune. Selune has many faces, just as the moon has it phases from waning to waxing. The world cycles through similar times of light and dark, good and evil, peace and turmoil. It was preached that if the scales tipped too far in the wrong direction, all life would be lost.

A verse in the scriptures I remember from my early youth is "If there is no darkness, not even the smallest shadow, the universe burns to ash. If there is no light, not even a single star in the sky, then all is lost in the darkness forever."

⊷⊙⊶

"People, people!" Elder Dorian shouts to the uneasy crowd, "No war will reach us; we are safe within our walls, guarded by the tower."

There murmuring stops, just for a moment, before picking up again even louder. I back towards the exit, skeptical of Elder Dorian's ability to calm the crowd. We've never seen a conflict this important before.

A member of the crowd shoves his way through the mass of people to confront the Elders. "How do you know?! Travelers tell us that city after city has been utterly destroyed, we're next!"

The crowd begins to yell and shout louder than before as the internal turmoil grows within these people.

‹‹• ‹•› ••›

The townspeople quickly lose faith in the balance the Elders tried so hard to keep. They started preparing for the worst. A militia was formed, and they started to manufacture weapons for those who could defend HighTower from the armies that would come. Only the gods knew what was coming. Eventually, even some priests and other guards joined the people; losing sight of the balance they swore to keep. Looking back, I suppose I should've cared more about that.

The dark armies were indeed coming, and the influence of evil had infected the townspeople, the guards, the priests, and eventually even some of the Elders. Shockingly, Elder Marialynn was first to denounce the order altogether to stand with those who wanted to defend themselves, but she wasn't the last.

⏸ ⊙ ⏸

"Dorian!" Elder Marialynn shouts at Elder Dorian, "You're a fool to think we'll be safe."

I stop before turning the corner into the corridor the Elders were crossing through, focusing on their conversation as it echoed off the stone walls.

"Maria—" Elder Dorian tried to speak.

"We will be slaughtered if we don't do anything, we should've been preparing for war a long time ago. We should be fighting on the front lines; we could've defeated them already!"

"Marialynn!" it is the first time I've ever heard Elder Dorian raise his voice, "You know the scripture; you know our cause. This isn't our fight."

A tearing sound tells me that Marialynn had ripped away her Elder's medallion, followed by the metallic clank as she tossed it to the ground. "This isn't *your* fight."

I turn and walk the other way, wanting to get away from the argument, but I look back to see Marialynn storming around the corner I had been hiding, heading away from me. Elder Dorian appeared, looking down at the forsaken medallion, now in his hand, disappointment and sorrow marring his face.

◄‖ ⊙ ‖►

The balance was eventually lost when we could feel the rumble of a massive army approaching from beyond the horizon. Most of the male townspeople set off to fight the looming threat. Many of the guards, fallen priests, and Elders went with them to fight. Those who stayed tried to maintain peace and calm, but to no avail. I could see the influence this evil had on everyone around me. This might've been the tipping point of balance for HighTower.

One fateful night, in the midst of a nightmare, the evil perpetrated even my own mind. I woke from my sleep in a sweat, struck with a fear I never before felt. I could hear the militia readying themselves for battle, and the distant roars of the approaching army. They had been coming for so long, and now they were here; this town would become a distant memory in the history of the world.

⇇ ⊙ ⇉

BOOM! Krakakakoom!

My eyes burst open, and I fall from my bed, shaking as the battle begins. I cover my face with my hands, feeling sweat running down my forehead.

"Where is everybody?" I ask aloud, almost whimpering in fright.

I try to stand; only to fall again as something shakes the earth under me. *Krakoom!* Faint shrieks from outside begin to enter my ears; bloody screams of murder.

The rumbling becomes ear-ringing loud. I rush to a storage closet and rummage around to pull out a spear for my self-defense. I clutch the wooden handle hard as I attempt to prepare myself to meet my demise at the hands of a nightmare.

BOOM! An explosion shakes the earth beneath my feet and collapses some furniture in my room. Fear tears through any bravery I had summoned. The spear clatters to the ground, slipping from my hands.

Fight, an unholy voice whispers to me, *die with them!* The voice cackles into silence.

Trembling sets in, the sweat gets worse. *BOOM!* My ears ring from the shockwave propagating through the stone around me. Like an animal, I crawl into the closet, awaiting my demise behind this closed door.

— Sam, The Unsung —

◄◄ ⊙ ►►

The armies had raided the living quarters, murdering those who had been guarding the innocent. Their efforts were futile, and innocent blood was shed by these monsters of darkness. They called out for help; I can still hear their screams echo through the halls and alleyways of everywhere I travel to.

I waited for silence to signify the armies had passed by, and harrowing silence did come. I was convinced that my death awaited me; certain that beyond the closet door was nothing but doom. I waited for it to come for many days. Hunger gnawed at my resolve to remain hidden. Occasionally, the roar of beasts and thud of footsteps convinced me to stay hidden just a bit longer.

◈

My breathing slows as footsteps come closer. A language unknown to me is spoken beyond a fallen wall. It's the same speech spoken by nearly every beast that passes by. These must be the grotesque beasts of the rumors, the Orcs.

Two distinct voices enter the room where I am hiding; their footsteps rummage through the stones and dirt that litter the floor. One mutters to the other, and their voices and steps come closer to my position. They come closer and closer shaking my once stoic nerves to tremors and heavy breathing.

Then, I hear a shout from one of them and *BANG!* An Orc is thrust into the door, and the sound of steel slicing through flesh is followed by a *THUD!* How could any being be so bloodthirsty that it would murder its own comrade?

The remaining beast begins to laugh to the sound of coins jingling together, and it walks away; away from me.

◈

That was the last sign of the armies of darkness. I remained in that closet for another day or two, just to ensure I was not found. Hunger finally drove me mad, forcing me to emerge, to find that every usable resource had been stolen. Horses and weapons were gone or desecrated. But the worst sight was that of what remained of the people I used to call my friends.

⊷⊙⊶

My body quivers, tears flowing down my cheeks. The atrocious smell of rotten decomposing flesh is nearly overpowering. My mind is completely empty, unable to comprehend what has happened. I feel nothing but disgust and overwhelming sadness.

I heave the door open, displacing the murdered Orc. As I emerge and take my first steps in days, I can only see the immense destruction caused by the battle I was too cowardly to fight and die alongside my comrades in.

Stone walls are knocked over, much of it ground into gravel, with only a few large stones left standing. Doors and furniture were burned to ash. This moment would mark the beginning of my journey; this new chapter of my life—my new life.

I step around the boulders that used to be this home of mine, walking into the gutted hallways, only to find a worse horror. A body had been left, its limbs torn away, and its face missing. I could see the blood splattered around, and footsteps walking away from the savage desecration in all directions. My hand reaches out to him as I choke out a sound, and begin to cry again.

"No," I tell myself, pulling back from the sight, "Leave."

My feet begin to shuffle away, and I comply with their will. I shamble away, quickly turning it into a run. Sprinting away, out of the hallway, passing body after body; blood pool after blood pool.

"How could I ever let this happen?" my thoughts interrogate me.

I run until I pass through the final doorway to outside, without a single thought of what lies before me. The shredded, blood-stained door swings open as I collide with it, and I fall face-first into wet gravel. The stench of the dead grows ever stronger.

❰❰ ⊙ ❱❱

The horrors of that would be unspeakable to most, but I relive these moments in my dreams. I hear the screams of the dying in the depths of my memory. Blood stains my hands for all eternity.

I laid there in the gravel, seemingly weeping for hours. I was too afraid—am too afraid, to look up at the corpses of those I called friends, mentors, and equals. Even though it wasn't courage that lifted me from the ground, I knew I had to face this; face my mistakes.

❰❰ ⊙ ❱❱

Slowly, I dig my hands into the ground and push myself up. My head still hangs in shame. But nonetheless, I rise. I force myself to see unspeakable horrors beyond my worst nightmares. I could hear the faint sounds of the dark army moving away to the west. The sound is that of doom and death for all that cross its path.

I look to see the bodies of innocent people scattered about the ground. Some are embedded into the fallen stone walls that made up homes, stables, or shrines. Some were burned, their flesh blackened and crumbling, but their bones remained to be consumed by the animals that are bound to come.

I see women and children, their bodies torn apart. Innards are sprawled about on the ground, and bite marks mar the bodies, chunks of flesh nowhere to be found. None were spared, not even the animals; every single horse is riddled with arrows and spears, the shafts protruding from all angles.

A mist begins to roll in from the north, obstructing my view any farther than the barbaric aftermaths, but they have already burned their mark in my mind.

Utterly defeated, I start away from the center of the carnage. I wander around HighTower in vain hopes of finding another survivor. I'm only greeted by crows and scavengers of the wild picking at rotten flesh. A sight I truly wish I had never stumbled upon creeps into my line of sight through the mist; a sight that will forever haunt me like none other.

I see the bodies of two Elders who were all too familiar to me; Elder Dorian and Elder Marialynn, one atop the other, dressed in their vestments. Elder Dorian had tried to sacrifice himself, but something had not only pierced through him but also through Elder Marialynn, leaving gaping voids in their bodies. Tears roll down my face when I look to see the medallion in Elder Dorian's hand; the medallion that was thrown to the ground and deformed against the stone.

⊪ ⊙ ⊫

I buried them, the two Elders. Their graves were placed side by side with the medallion buried with Elder Marialynn. I had spent the week, dawn till dusk, burying every dead body I could find. The graves were shallow, and close together; their final resting places in the forests around HighTower.

After I had completed the burials and my prayers, I gathered some things as I prepared to leave HighTower; leave that place to rest. I had gathered what few weapons and vestments that had survived. I even found a small pouch of money, among other things.

I headed east, into the wilderness but in the opposite direction of that the dark army had gone. I traveled for days to find another civilization. The days turned to weeks as I hunted and scavenged for food. I had nothing for a companion but regret. My hunger couldn't be satiated, my thirst never quenched. My dreams were haunted by the things I've seen. Those weeks probably turned to months; I had lost count, but my axes were dulling. Over that time, though, I honed my skills for animal tracking and basic survival.

It took a long time before I encountered another creature smarter than a beast. I had started to lose hope, after so much time of finding no other settlements, nor these other species I heard so many stories of. One day, I finally crossed paths with a group of creatures I'd never heard story of. They identified themselves as Gnomes. Communication was subpar, but they did speak my native language of Rillish.

They told me they had been traveling for many days, searching for resources to bring back to their village, and that I was welcome to travel with them.

◄╫ ⊙ ╫►

"You are human? Yes?" the oldest Gnome asks me, "What is your name?"

"My name is Sam," I reply.

"You seem like nice guy, travel among us, please."

I bow to him in thanks, and I change my course to match their southwesterly route. We start walking again, following a river.

There was a small child among the ten or so Gnomes, this child couldn't've been older than four. He enjoys making funny faces and pulling on my leggings. I didn't pay too much attention to the child.

"Where you from, Sam?" another Gnome asks me.

Memories of horrors from HighTower begin to flash before me. My eyes dart around seeing people dying around me, and my breathing turns into hyperventilation. Suddenly, it stops when the female Gnome says something in her language.

"You don't have to tell," she assures me, "My name Tazmyre." She pats my leg and we begin to walk again.

They were a fine bunch of Gnomes, very welcoming. Over the couple days travel, I had learned a few words from the child, who was surprisingly literate. They brought me to their village.

The villagers were very skeptical of a human entering the village. I was told of other humans over the hundreds of years who only sought weapons of war from the diminutive people.

⏸ ⊙ ⏸

Caltor and a village guard, not so different a profession from me, begin to argue about something in their language. They begin to shout, and the village guard begins to angrily point at me.

Tazmyre tugs on my leggings to talk to me. "Gnome here don't like humans. They only come to us for, uh—" she makes a *Boom* noise with the according hand motions, "So we don't let humans in. *Usually.*"

The guard begins to rubs the bridge of his nose and unlocks the gate to let us in, he whispers something in Gnomish as I walk past him, bending down underneath the low gate.

Many of the Gnomes looked at me with concern. I could tell they didn't want me there. Time changed that; I stayed with the Gnomes for many months. They helped me heal a little and forget the horrific aftermath of the slaughter at HighTower. I learned their language, making it easier to speak with them.

Many of the Gnomes realized I was only seeking reconciliation, not war. After that, they welcomed me into their society. I learned many things while I was there, like how to properly handle animals instead of simply tracking them for food. Bending low to enter doorways became second nature for me.

One Gnome, in particular, was very fond of me. Her name was Miara, and she worked at a market selling food. Naturally, I frequented her shop often.

Over time, I felt a pull to leave this village, and travel once more. Before I left, they gifted me supplies and maps for my journey. I do miss them. Miara had written me a poem before I left. I've lost the parchment it was written on long ago, but this poem was a light amongst all the darkness that kept hold of my mind.

◂‖ ⊙ ‖▸

"Sam!" I hear someone call out. I turn to see through the main gate Miara, running to me. I stop to wait as she comes closer and closer.

"Sam! I have a gift for you," she tells me, handing me a small rolled up piece of parchment tied up with a red piece of silk.

I happily accept the paper and begin to place it in my bag, only to be greeted by a tight hug from her around my abdomen. It's a strange feeling, having someone show any sort of affection. If she, if any of them, knew what I did, I'd be a disgrace.

She releases her grip and runs back into the village, and I begin on my way, keeping the parchment in my hand.

◀╫ ⊙ ╫▶

Hopefully, I will always remember that poem. It read in Rillish:

"This is Sam, an Unsung; a victim of war and loss.
One who has truly seen pain.
This is Sam, whose faith never waned.
Who would never let life be tossed away.
For this is Sam, *the* Unsung."

As ironic as the poem is, it is one of the lights that fights my trauma. It fights for remembrance against my dead people. While traveling, I turned to scripture; I read them over and over again to try and truly understand what it is I used to stand for and hope to stand for when my journey is finished.

Traveling led me from town to town. I decided to help those in need in whatever ways I could. As I became more and more capable, the things I did to help those around me grew truly heroic in the eyes of others. Most of the time, the people were unable to pay me for my deeds, so instead, they offered me places to rest my head or food for me to eat. Such wonderful people. On two separate occasions, I hunted down beasts terrorizing villages or travelers. I was gifted a sword and some chainmail armor, respectively.

⊷ ⊙ ⊶

A cold wind blows from the northeast, bringing along pestering insects and the birds riding the currents. I focus on the sounds around me, listening for the beast. The townspeople described it as a boar-like creature that would attack people traveling the roads connecting this town to a larger city, and occasionally attack livestock.

The smell of dung from the forest animals is usually ambient, but there was an unusual smell leading to this patch of woods, along with some tracks. Bushes rustle as if something brushed past them, and I quickly crouch to the ground to avoid being seen.

Suddenly, a loud grunt and roar emanate from behind a tree, and the following beast begins to run out into the open, perhaps chasing something. I ready my hand axe, waiting for an opportune moment to strike.

FOOSH! The axe digs into the side of the boar; it's not dead, but very angry. The beast reorients itself to find me, and begins to charge in my direction.

I ready my second axe, aiming for the head; waiting for the right moment to launch the sharpened steel…

FOOSH! The beast's legs lose stability, and it falls to the ground, sliding in the dirt and mud.

"Finally, I caught you," I whisper to it, "I've been tracking you for days."

I pull my axes out of the lifeless beast, and slide them back into their holsters at my sides. A gust of wind blows the strong scent of the forest life into my face and rustles the leaves of the foliage.

"Time to take you back to the village."

As I traveled, I often found myself in saloons, drinking mugs full of water and listening in on the conversations and stories being told around me. I learned that the war had ended from a drunken man cursing the dark army, before promptly falling unconscious. I learned the name of the leader of the dark army during a similar experience weeks later.

❮❙ ☉ ❙❯

"Damn that Asharak!" A drunken man cries out.

A waiter walks up to try and calm him down, and I go back to my reading. I'm promptly distracted by the man shouting once more.

"His army destroyed my home!" he yells, "Damn him!"

The waiter pushes him back down to his seat. "You need to calm down, you're causing a ruckus."

The man starts crying, and rests his head on the counter of the table he's at. I once again go back to my reading.

❮❙ ☉ ❙❯

I learned much about the history of Rillanon by listening in to people talk, but stories of Asharak were few and far between. Some say he transcended death multiple times, others say he was just a crazed mage. I'm certain that he is the one who laid waste to the land; to my beloved home. I swore to myself that I would find him one day and avenge my people, and all others that were slain during his war.

I suppose that that journey ended a while ago, and I started a new one during another day spent with water at the bar. A fight broke out, and I had decided to fetch a sacred item from a fallen city for a traveler, and two elves decided to follow me.

⇇ ⊙ ⇉

A strange traveler begins to talk with the owner of the Axe &
Thistle, the local tavern. He begs for a place to stay for him and his
village as it was recently burned by bandits. He spoke of soil that was
blessed by the Goddess of the Harvest herself, and it needed to be
retrieved so he and his people could start anew somewhere else.

"I will go and retrieve your dirt, in what direction is your village?"
I ask him.

"Oh thank you, good Sir," he replies, "It's to the west, but I'm
afraid it's been overrun by bandits."

I turn away before he finishes, and begin to walk the path to
fulfill the needs of this man.

A female elf and her companion begin to chase me. "Hey! Wait
up, you're not going alone!" she shouts. No matter if they follow me, I will
go and do.

When we arrived, we were met with a terrible sight; one all too
familiar to me. Bodies littered the ground with flames still burning. We
labored the day gathering the bodies and cremating them, whilst I said a
prayer for the dead. A female dwarf, of an Order of Solare, the God of
the Sun, met us while she was sent on a similar mission from her order.

Rythlen decided to join us that day in our travels. Later, an Orc named Throck joined us as well. I couldn't save him; may he rest in peace. A druid also joined us trying to find the culprit behind a possessed and corrupted boar she tended to when we met. We pursue one called the Accuser, whom I believe to be Asharak, to bring balance in the land once more.

I believe that one day, balance will be restored, and my people avenged. In this mission I may die, but so be it if I do.

For I am Sam, the Unsung.

The Study of Things Beyond Our Understanding

❖

C*LICK, CLICK.* I hurry to light my last cigarette before they take them and basically strip me naked, all before I'm allowed inside. Alas, I see someone coming out from the door to the docking station.

"Sir, you are not allowed to smoke here!" he shouts, speedily walking towards me and my escort.

"Told you," my escort says, holding out his hand.

Reluctantly, I hand over the lighter and cigarettes.

"Welcome, sir," the man says, "And you are?"

"I'm Scott Dike; here on behalf of the U.S. government," I introduce myself, "I'm here to make sure that this is still a worthy investment for government funds."

"Ah, yes," he says, signaling for all of us to come into the facility, "I expect you enjoyed your flight?"

"Hardly... I just spent six damn months in space, and I missed my kid's soccer game."

"Well, nobody's first time is the best time."

I pull out my clipboard to see a checklist of things I'm supposed to ask. "So, uh, explain to me why we should keep funding this?"

"Oh, I'm not the person to ask for that, you'll want to talk to one of the main physicists. I'm just janitorial duty at the moment."

"Well, I'd like to talk to them ASAP."

"First, we'll need to prep you to enter into the inner facility."

They lead me in, scrub me down, and give me new clothes that I needed someone to help me into. But they did give me a cool lab coat that I'm sure my kids will love.

"I talked with Doctor Hills, he said he'd like to show you around personally, so I'll take you to him." the janitor tells me.

We make our way down several elevators, until we get to the bottom. There, I can feel things are different; things are heavier, and a little more on edge.

"Hello, Mr. Dike!" another lab-coated man with glasses says to me. Definitely looks the Doctor type, with graying hair and wide eyes.

"Doctor Hills?" I ask.

"The only one on this vessel," he jokes, "Let me show you around."

He leads us down one more level, where things really feel different. "I've been informed that you're the one to make sure this project is worth funding, correct?"

"Yes," I say, pulling out my new plastic clipboard, "First thing on my list, is how far over budget have you gone?"

"Oh, not at all, we're actually under budget."

"Really?" I ask, checking off a box.

"Oh yes."

"And what you've learned, does it have any military, commercial, or civil use?"

"We've been running experiments on waste disposal and energy production, and the results are promising."

"I'm looking for results, Doctor, no promises."

"Mmn, let's say that each pound of waste disposed of equates to enough power to run the city of Las Vegas for six months."

"Now those are results!"

"I'd like to show you in person what exactly we're studying."

"Singularly, or something of the sort, if I can remember."

"*Singularities*, Black Holes."

"Right, just show me so I can leave and go home."

"Very well."

He leads down level after level. My feet feel heavier and it feels my head is weightless. Finally, he says we're as close as we can be without special equipment.

"The gravity engines are only at fifty percent, so gravity is a little more, uh, wonky," the doctor tells me. He leads me to a computer monitor and pressure pipe with a clear pipe cover on the end.

"Please, take a look," he offers.

I wobble over to the computer monitor, and it's just black with a lot of ghosting on the screen. "There's nothing here, it's just black."

He chuckles, "That's sort of the point. Take a look down the pipe."

I move over and support myself on the pipe. I look down and there's a large glass lens with utter blackness. Nothingness. The pipe is fully lit, but it's pitch black at the bottom.

"It's so dark."

"You're staring directly into the most powerful beast in the entire universe. A Black Hole."

Under the Contra

⊰◎⊱

THE WIND BLOWS, the sounds of gravel shifting as it fills the graves is the only things reaching my ears, and the long shadows cast by the westward setting sun make their way to my sight. I'm the last one; there is no one else to tend to the farm and the animals.

I shovel the last of the dirt on top of my family's remains and head off to make sure the animals are fed. One step at a time makes life's journey, whether it be feeding animals or overcoming the loss of my family.

Family stories from generations past speak of Eden, and the garden hidden within. It's the cradle where humanity was created and made its first mistakes. I must travel there at some point; it was going to be a rite of passage with my father and my eldest brother.

But now I'm alone, and there is no one to tend to the farm or the animals. It was disease that took them; it swept the land, taking my family and some of the animals. Father used to tell me it was to cleanse the world of the wicked.

I dump some of the feed in front of the animals and head to home for the night, hoping to dream a good dream. The bed is cold and the night is silent without my brothers and sisters.

My mind slips into slumber, and I begin to dream of the city of Eden. I dream that it's a beautiful city, full of trees and foliage blooming with sweet smells. Luxurious clothing and adornments made of gold.

A loud sound wakes me from the slumber. The animals begin calling out in fear, and something hits their water supply. I can hear the rushing water spilling around the ground. I regain my faculties and put on a robe.

I look outside the window to see robbers of the night attempting to coerce the asses to their will. I grab my blade and rush to the animals. On my way, an animal kicks open the gate just enough to let a few animals out.

"Hey! You there!" I shout out, running to them with blade in hand. They're Cainites, descendants of the first murderer.

They run to hide inside the swine's stable, and I march on inside. They're huddled in the corner with only their eyes reflecting the moon's light.

"Why are you here?" I demand. They all huddle closer together and start whispering.

"Hey!" I shout again.

A young Cainite girl comes out among them and kneels before me. "I'm sorry, I'm sorry," she says, "We're just looking for horses to—"

I cry out in anger and swing my blade into the wooden post constructing the doorway. "What horses!?" I yell, "I'm a farmer, why would I have a horse?

"A horse can't pull a plow; a horse can't haul seed! Why would a farmer have a horse?!"

She starts crying and puts her hands above her head, begging for forgiveness. I didn't realize a Cainite ever would do this.

"Go away," I command them, "Leave me be."

"We're just trying to go to Eden, please," she begs.

"Why would Cainites go to Eden?" I ask, "Why not just return to Enoch."

"Eden is on the way to Enoch, so please help us."

I do eventually need to go to Eden and abandon this farm. My family's gone, and they're not ever going to come back. This farm was theirs, and now they're gone.

Another one of the Cainites points at me, saying, "You must know the way to Eden. Show us!"

"Why would I show you the way to Eden?" I retort.

"You're all alone," he tells me, "So you can show us."

His words hurt, reminding me of the void my family used to fill. The abyss I feel eats away at everything surrounding it, leaving a charcoal silhouette of what used to be.

I wish to utter curses through my teeth, but he is right. I'm alone here, and I'll die here too if I don't go. Why trust Cainites, though? They're thieves, robbers, even murderers.

I turn away into the night and stare at the plains and fields that go off into the black horizon, only distinguished by heaven shining through the sky. Somewhere, beyond the horizon, awaits Eden and the garden therein.

I look back at the Cainites huddling in the corner in fear; these are the very incarnate of the devil on Earth?

"Why do you want to journey to Eden?" I ask, "I don't think they'll welcome you with open arms considering your legacy."

The youngest of the four Cainites jumps up to his feet. "I wish to bathe in the rivers of the garden, and become white as snow!"

The older of the female Cainites grabs him by his garments and pull the boy back to them. "You really believe the rivers can do that?"

"It's rumored that anything from the Garden removes the legacy of Cain from us," she says, "Although, most of our people don't think it's a blessing."

"Show us the way," another one of them says.

Show us the way he demands. What do I have to lose?

⫻ ⊙ ⫸

Today, the sun will rise on my home, and set in the wilderness. Of everything my life could've been, it's traveling with a band of Cainites to Eden. Eden is eastward of here, so we began traveling when the sun shines through my window.

"So which way is Eden?" One of them asks me.

"It's to the East, where the sun rises," I reply, "I thought all Cainites live in Enoch."

"Actually I was born north of here," the older of the female Cainites tells me, "My family were nomads, traveling to greener pastures."

"I didn't know Cainites held to their family units," I remark.

She looks away in shame or of something else. I walk up to the gate keeping the animals in their place, everything my father and his fathers worked for, and release the gate and the animals kept inside. "Let us go now," I declare.

We begin traveling east, onward to the legendary city of our ancestors. Our path was clear, with only tall grasses at our feet; we traveled in silence until the sunset in the west and the land went dark to make way to the heavens to shine.

I can still see the faint glow of my home in the distance. I could still turn back, but what would I be returning to? My thoughts drift into dreams of Eden. These dreams aren't so sweet though, it's of poverty and evil; of natural men.

The warmth of the sun touches my face and brings me out of my dreams. I look around to see the two youngest Cainites still sleeping, but the older two sitting together weaving together the tall grass into decorations.

I sit up and begin to roll my blanket up. "How did you sleep?" the girl asks.

"Just fine, yourself?" I say out of habit.

"Very well," she replies, "This ground is very soft."

I disregard and tie up my sandals. "What is your name?" she asks.

"Jonathan, son of Michael," I tell her, "What are yours'?"

"I am Awan, and these are my two brothers Laval and Mathusal," she tells me, pointing at the boy next to her weaving the grass and sleeping child, "and the young girl is my father's sister's daughter."

"Pleasure to make your acquaintance," Laval greets me.

I clear my throat as I finish packing my provisions. "We should begin traveling again; it's not good to travel to Eden in the dark."

"But they are still sleeping," Awan tells the obvious.

"But we can't just sleep all day or we'll never make it to Eden."

Laval starts a coughing spell and quickly subsides, but it's loud enough to wake the sleeping children. Awan pushes on his arm in retaliation.

The two children slowly come to consciousness and roll around in the flattened grass. Awan crawls over to cradle them. I've always been told that Cainites are savages and murderers and thieves, but Awan's so gentle as she holds the two children.

They take a little time to stretch, but they have no provisions to pack. We take another day's journey in relative silence. The grass has become less tall and overgrown bushes begin to dot the landscape.

Grass turns to dirt as the bushes grow taller and wider as the sun dances across the sky down into the west. Laval starts another coughing spell and Awan sets her hand on his back until his coughing subsides.

The sun sets beneath the western horizon and we stop for the night. The two children fall asleep quickly with Laval following suit. The crawling things begin their nightly songs all over one another.

"My family, we traveled all the time, never making a home," Awan tells me as I lay down on my mat, "Our caravan only had maybe twenty people."

I try to ignore and fall asleep, but she starts to talk again. "What about your family? Where are they?"

I finally respond after a few more moments of silence, "They died, my family. My father returned from a journey, and sickness killed them one night after a long time of suffering."

"I'm sorry," she consoles me.

"Now let me sleep, we'll start again in the morning," I command, drifting off into the aether of my dreams.

⊶⊙⊷

Our travels have led us into a forest, one my father spoke of in his many travels. He told us outlandish tales of the beasts that creep within, but I'm afraid all of his tales were told for small children and hide the true monsters that prey.

We all stop for a moment at the borders of the forest. I rummage through my bad and pull out my blade in preparation of what might lay before us.

"My father spoke of this forest, there should be a settlement on the other side," I tell them, "We need to stay close."

Laval starts a coughing spell and wipes away some fluid from his mouth. A doe prances across an open space of the forest and we begin to proceed into the trees.

Thankfully, there is a clear path that's been set by travelers of the previous generations, but I'm still wary. I try my hardest to focus on my surroundings, listening to the rustling of the leaves and branches, the bellows of the wind.

Laval begins his coughing spells, but this time it's coarse and forceful. Awan huddles the two children and Laval begins to stumble. Suddenly, I feel a dangerous presence falling upon us.

The forest becomes silent and the wind slows as heavy footsteps creep towards us. A low purr shakes me to the bone as I perch my blade up high in preparation. Laval kneels down and Awan huddles the two children.

Two bushes are pushed to the side as a great big cat marches through them in confidence. Laval throws a stone at the big cat's face, shifting its attention to him while I swing my blade up into the throat. Awan lifts the children and starts running down the path and Laval makes his way behind me.

The beast drips blood from its wound and starts to cough blood onto the ground. I push Laval down the path and follow Awan in running.

Wounded, the beast tries to follow us. It runs faster and faster as the blood dries on its throat. Laval starts falling behind Awan and I stop in my tracks to face the beast again. It jumps aloft ready to pounce on me, but a stone from Laval strikes it in eye and I thrust my sickle into its throat once more.

The big cat's immense weight crushes down on me, but the beast has been struck dead.

⇇ ⊙ ⇉

I bite into the fire-roasted flesh of the beast. The night falls upon us, trapping us in the midst of thick forests until the dawn. Feasting upon flesh was often saved for special occasions, days of special thanks; today we are grateful for our lives.

Laval stares at the food in his hand, whilst Awan and the two siblings feast along with me. Laval has become increasingly sick during our journey. "What is the true reason you all seek the Eden's river?"

Mathusal jumps to his feet and exclaims, "To become white as snow! To be pure!"

Awan smiles, "Those not of Cain's lineage don't take lightly to us, we're often shunned. The rivers purify those who enter into its waters and will remove Cain's curse from us. Why do you seek the waters?"

"My family dreamed of sending me and my eldest brother to Eden, as a pilgrimage to God."

"So you don't seek the waters?"

I shake my head. "Laval, why do you seek the waters?"

"I wish to protect my family, not to seek the waters."

"I never imagined family would be so important to you."

Laval sets his meat back into the fire. "There's much you don't know about us."

It's not long before their two siblings fall into a slumber. Soon after, I smother the fire and Laval lays down to sleep also.

"You've grown during our travels, you know," Awan tells me as I prepare my blanket.

"In what way?" I reply.

"I've seen you move past nearly everything you've thought about us, about Cainites."

"Is that so?" I ask.

"I think so," she says, "But Laval hasn't moved past his."

"So what about your family? What happened to them?"

"We were nomads, wandering from hill to hill. But I longed for adventure, and that brought danger to them. And so, they cast me out and my family followed me. Our father died from disease also."

"I'm sorry to hear that."

"We have nowhere to go to be accepted, so we seek the waters of Eden to purify us, so we can mingle with others and settle down."

"That's very noble."

◄╫ ⊙ ╫►

Exiting the forest led us to grasslands once again, and I can see the haze of a nearby settlement. It'll take an entire day, but we could replenish ourselves there, but we all agree to keep traveling. Laval, in particular, insisted to keep on our way despite his condition, so we continue across the landscape.

We traveled for days until the haze of the city faded beyond the horizon and we rested for another night. Mathusal and Abbin fall asleep, followed by Laval, Awan, and I. But it's not soon after that the autumn rains begin pouring down from the heavens.

The rain is cold and painful, like insects attacking your skin. This isn't good, someone could get sick, and we don't have any medicine. I rise from my sleeping mat and lift my head to the sky. *What are we going to do?*

Lights dance around the sky in fantastic shows with the loud applause of the hosts of heaven. I look over to see Awan holding her two younger siblings close.

"Do you not like it?" I ask her.

"No, the lightning scares them."

"Why?"

"We believe it to be the wrath of angels to punish the wicked."

"How curious. I've never heard that," I say, "My father always told me it was angels performing for each other."

Laval begins a coughing spell, but it's hoarse and deep. "How far are we?" he asks.

"We're still months away. We'll turn around to get you medicine."

"No," he demands, "We'll keep going."

"Laval—" Awan tries to say something, but Laval cuts her off.

"We'll keep going; shouldn't there be another town on the way there?"

"I wouldn't know. I only know which direction Eden's in."

"I'll take my chances, I don't want to get there any later than I have to," he continues to demand.

"Laval, it's only a few days—"

"I'm not going back!" he persists.

"Fine, but what do you want to do about tonight? We can't just sleep in that rain." I ask.

"This isn't our first time sleeping in the rain."

"Laval," Awan tenderly talks.

❙❙◉❙❙

The rain eventually stopped sometime in the morning, and after we removed enough mud from our things, we trekked on through the muddy grassland. Day after day after the rain, Laval's sickness progressed more and more. We were weeks away from any settlement, but we continued on.

We stop after the day's travels on some rocky formation surrounded by barren, hard landscape. I can see the amber glow of civilization off on the horizon, something we can arrive by tomorrow's end.

The sun sets and I start a fire to keep warm. Awan and her siblings were all so somber today, unlike any other day we've traveled together. Silently, we all arrange for sleeping on this formation. No dirt for stakes or comfort, but neither was there mud or grass to hide pests.

The night creeps on, but I keep myself aroused. I fantasize about Eden, the city of our first parents, the birth of civilization and what kind of wonders lie within. I've dreamt of Eden often; from angels mingling with men to the greed and destruction of sin, and I know not which one to believe.

I stare into the sky and wonder about the heavens painted onto it, when I hear something disturbs the fire pit. I look over to see Laval walk off with a torch, possibly to relieve himself in privacy. But I wait for him to return to no avail. I stand up to look into the distance and see the faint glow of his torch off into the distance from where we traveled.

I chase after him, calling to him, but he doesn't stray from his course. I run and run, but he continues on his way.

"Laval!" I shout, running through the dry landscape into the tall grass.

"Leave me alone, white man!" he cries back.

I sprint after him, "Laval! What are you doing?!" I catch up to him, and tackled him to the ground, tossing the torch somewhere in the grass. He pushes me away and tries to crawl into the tall grass.

"You wouldn't understand!" He says, "You're not one of us."

I grab him and pull him backward. Thunder cracks and lightning dances across the cloud floating above. "What wouldn't I understand, Laval?"

He shoves me away, throwing a pebble between my eyes. "You're not one of us, you'd never understand."

More lightning dances around and we become illuminated by burning grass. I try to pull him back, but he resists. "We've been traveling together for over a year, Laval. *Together!*"

The fire begins to rage, surrounding us. The wind storms, creating chaos. "Leave me to die! *Alone!*"

"No Laval!" I try to drag him away from the fire.

"Leave me be!" he kicks me away with both legs. As I fall to the ground, lightning strikes the ground between the two of us. Blinding light, deafening clap; the next thing I see is the sun rising with the blue sky scattered with gray clouds. As I come to, I recognize the sound of shoveling dirt over a corpse.

◂◂ ⊙ ▸▸

My eyes are flooded with light, there's a ringing in my ears. "What happened?" I ask, "Where is he?"

The ringing fades, revealing concords, but the concords fade as well leaving only the tears of grief. "Awan? Where are you?" I ask out.

"What happened here, Jonathan?" Awan asks me through tears.

The light begins to fade from my vision, showing me cloudy skies and a sad, broken family. "There was a storm, he was abandoning us. I was trying to bring him back; there was something bright."

"He was dying," She tells me, "That's why he wanted to go to Eden, to be healed. His affliction is passed down from father to firstborn, he wanted to be healed by the waters."

She collapses beside me, clutching my chest. She cries and cries.

⊷ ⊙ ⊶

We've been traveling in silence ever since Laval's death; it's been weeks and months we've been traveling since then. I've stopped dreaming, I feel no drive, but we carry on.

Finally, I see the landmark signifying Eden. My father told me stories, that every time he went, there was a magnificent tree. It bore no fruit, nor had leaves, but needles pointing to the heavens. I see it off in the distance.

Awan wraps her arm around mine, "That's it, isn't it? We've heard the stories of a tree that points to heaven."

"Yes, that's the tree," I tell her, "Eden lies behind the horizon."

We set up camp for the last time as the sun illuminates our destination. Awan huddled her two siblings and I watch as the sun slept in the west. I stared at heaven all night long, thinking of what truly lies in Eden. In our travels, I've seen the works of men, both good and evil, so what lies in the city of our first parents?

The sun peeks above the horizon in the east. Awan awakes from beside me and we get ready for the last day of our journey. As we travel to the tree, I see the haze of the city. The tree is dying. Its skin is falling away and the foretold needles are few and far between. Scattered about the ground are small saplings of different heights.

"Come on," I tell them, "We're almost there."

I pull on Awan's hand to bring them all along to our long-awaited destination. Eden is only a few hours away; we can all see the city. The two younger children dance around in joy and enjoying the lush greenery surrounding us. Soon we can hear the bustling of the people.

A young boy begins to wave both his hands at us in the distance, but the boy is swept away by someone else. All this time, and I don't know what to expect.

The closer we got the more averted eyes we received. As we walked through the crowds and the streets, very few people cast their gaze.

"I'm looking for the Garden," I ask around to multiple people, but they just shoo us away.

I walk up to an elderly person, sitting in a chair on the side of the road. "I'm looking for the Garden, can you help us?" I ask him.

He chuckles, "You're a traveler, I see. You'll find what you're looking for when you start seeing the priestguards.

"Where are you from?" he asks.

"We're from the west, from a family farm," I reply.

He chuckles again, "You've come very far from home."

"Yes, we've been traveling for a long time."

"Who have you been traveling with? I can't seem to recognize them."

Awan huddles the two children together from the crowd, keeping them by her side. "Four Cainites, we came here together."

"Are you Cainite?" he asks, "I'm blind; I can't quite see you clearly."

"No," I tell him.

"How unusual," he says, "I don't think I've ever met someone who travels without his own. Nonetheless, I hope you find what you're looking for."

"Thank you, you're very kind," Awan tells him.

⊶⊙⊷

I see a group of young and old men, all dressed in similar attire; they're all dressed in white robes with eccentric patterns trailing around the edges. Some of them are even holding spears.

"Are-Are you the priestguards?" I ask aloud to them.

Many of them look at us, and then turn away. "We're looking for the Garden, can you help us."

A young man walks up to us, stopping us from coming any closer. "They're not to come any closer,'" he tells me, pointing to Awan and the two children, "The Garden's gone, now go on your way."

"Onde," an elderly man approaches as us, "All are welcome."

The young man shrugs the man's hand off his shoulder, "The Garden's gone, now take the cursed ones and leave Eden," he shouts at us.

"Onde! Go over there and attend to your post," the man commands him. Reluctantly, the young man leaves.

"I apologize for him," the man continues, "But I'm afraid the Garden was taken many, many generations ago back to heaven. Here, the priestguards guard where the gates would be out of tradition. I'm afraid what you're looking for is now gone."

I look behind him to see two of the priestguard facing away from each other on either sides of an alter. "My father told me there was a river nearby, one that ran through the Garden."

The man pauses to think, "There is a river nearby, but I'm afraid I can't tell whether or not it used to run through the Garden of Eden."

He gave us directions to the river and sent us on our way. We spent the entire day traveling; we left the city and traveled into the nearby wilderness. The river gave life to the earth around it. We found fish and small animals and many pests.

Awan sits down into the river and takes a handful of water to drink. The two children sit beside her. I stand underneath a tree in the shade from the sun.

"The water tastes good, at least," she tells me.

"Is it everything you dreamt of?" I ask Awan.

"I think I found something better in the journey," she says looking at me, smiling.

"Me too," I reply, smiling back at her.

When The Shadows Disappear

❮❮◎❯❯

MOMENTS TURN from seconds to minutes, as I'm here to contemplate my entire existence, all in the time it takes for an atom to break open. Perhaps I should've been a better person, giving more to the poor. Maybe ask my coworker to lunch.

But all of that ends. My shadow becomes sharper and longer, stretching out in front of me between all the travelers, I should've worked harder in my job; maybe then I'd have a raise and be on a business trip right now. Maybe it's the passion burning inside me, warming me up. Perhaps I'll go home, wake up and work longer hours tomorrow.

This briefcase my grandfather made just for me as a tradition for us getting a stable desk job away from the war. It's getting a little too heavy for me these days; I've been carrying all my documents so I can double check them after hours.

There must be gum on my shoes, they feel like they're sticking to the ground with each stride I take to make sure I'm home to feed my pet on time, he gets mad when I'm late and I can't take him for a walk around the neighborhood before dinner and slumber.

I can feel death approaching me from behind, it's a very warm evening and it seems there's glass all over the ground. This suit was a gift from my brother; I'd hate to ruin it. We used to visit each other once a week before work got too busy and we'd play tennis.

How long has it been already? My shadow has disappeared and my watch stopped ticking, so I can't tell the time anymore. I turn to see if everyone is also frozen by the inevitable doom, but all I see is the sun setting right over downtown.

⊩⊙⊪

Special Thanks

The UNLV Society of Creative Writers
Brendan K.
Cameron P.
Cian M.
Colton S.
Emi K.
Job V.
Nancy N.
Rachel P.

⊷⊙⊶

In Memoriam Of

Megan & Lola

Thank You

Thank you for reading.

The End.